TEN MINUTES

OATH KEEPERS MC

WALL STREET JOURNAL & USA TODAY BESTSELLING AUTHOR

SAPPHIRE KNIGHT

Sapphire Knight

Ten Minutes

Oath Keepers MC

Wall Street Journal & USA Today Bestselling Author

Sapphire Knight

Copyright 2022 Sapphire Knight

All Rights Reserved

Editing by Swish Design & Editing

Warning

Warning: This novel includes graphic language and adult situations. It may be offensive to some readers and includes situations that may be hotspots for certain individuals. This book is intended for ages 17 and older due to steamy, sexy, and hotness that will have you jumping your man. This work is fictional. The story is meant to entertain the reader and may not always be completely accurate. Any reproduction of these works without Author Sapphire Knight's written consent is pirating and will be punished to the fullest extent of the law. Stealing this book makes you a thieving prick, and I hope your tits fall off.

This book is fiction.

The guys are over-the-top alphas.

My men and women are nuts.

This isn't real.

Don't steal my shit, I have bills too.

Read for enjoyment.

This isn't your momma's cookbook.

Easily offended people shouldn't read this.

Don't be a dick.

Blurb

Ten minutes was all it took for me to know she was meant to be mine. The scared woman was running from something and seeing her in that hospital bed solidified my feelings. I wasn't ever letting her go, I'd protect her, covet her, and claim her baby as mine.

Naomi would never have to be frightened again and if the demons chasing her ever showed up, she wouldn't fight them alone. I've been known to have a soft spot for women in distress, and she's no different. Only this time around, I'm willing to give her my property patch, not just my heart.

Club Tree:

(Charter, Road Name, Position, Ol' Lady, Nickname, Kids, Book Title)

Oath Keepers/Widow Makers hybrid charter:

Viking – President (Prez),

Heir to the Widow Makers MC, previous NOMAD,

Princess aka Cinderella - ol' lady (Princess)

One of the twin babies

Odin – Vice President (VP), Viking's younger blood brother,

previous Widow Maker, Cherry - ol' lady (Cherry)

One of the twin babies

Torch – Death Dealer (Punisher/Enforcer), Caspian Teague

previous Widow Maker, grew up with Viking,

Laura aka Flame – ol' lady,

Annabelle - daughter

Saint and Sinner – Hell Raisers, previous NOMADS,

Jude aka Baby - ol' lady (Baby)

Nightmare – Good friend to Viking and Exterminator,

club officer, previous NOMAD, Bethany aka Daydream - ol' lady,

Maverick – son (Daydream)

Blaze – Viking's cousin and Princess' security,

previous Widow Maker

Amelia aka Teach – ol' lady (Heathen)

6

Ten Minutes

Chaos – Close with the NOMADS, Ex-NFL football player,

Hollywood – ol' lady,

Kadence – daughter (Freight Train),

Trixie - daughter (Hollywood)

Smokey – Treasurer, previous Widow Maker

Mercenary – Transfer from Chicago Charter,

Chevelle aka Chevy - ol' lady,

Hemi, Nova, Shelby – son and daughters (Chevelle)

Frost – Newest patched member, Bronx's blood brother

Karma – Prospect, twin to Rage

Rage – Prospect, twin to Karma

Scot – Deceased

Bronx – Deceased

NOMADS:

Exterminator

Ruger

Spider

Knuckle Buster

Magnum

Original Oath Keepers MC:

Ares – Prez, Avery - ol' lady (Forsaken Control)

Cain – VP, London - ol' lady, Jamison Cade – son (Exposed)

2 Piece – Gun Runner – SAA, Avery - ol' lady (Relinquish)

Sapphire Knight

Twist – Unholy One, Sadie aka Sadie Baby - ol' lady, Cyle – son (Friction)

Spin – Treasurer, Naomi – ol' lady - (Ten Minutes)

Snake – Previous president's son, Peppermint - ol' lady (Sweet Surrender)

Capone – Deceased

Smiles – Deceased

Shooter – Deceased

Scratch – Deceased

Rivals

Iron Fists MC

Twisted Snakes MC

Mexican Cartel

CHAPTER ONE

Spin

After I say my goodbyes to the brothers, I head out front and climb on my bike. It's too damn chilly to be riding the fucking thing, but I'm holding out for as long as possible. At this rate, in the middle of December, my fingers will freeze off and I won't be able to ride, no matter how stubborn I attempt to be. Bad enough my ears feel like icicles resting on my head, as my tall mohawk offers me zero warmth. It's all for the badass look and no practicality. My brothers are just as stubborn as I am about the winter months, not trading their bikes in for the cages unless there's ice on the road. I shouldn't complain, being that Texas is one of the warmest places to live in the winter months.

With a twist of the handle, my bike roars to life. The vibrations rush through me and instantly set my mind at peace. Tom Petty blares from my speakers, singing about free falling. I listen to a little bit of everything. I always have, but lately, I've been on a classic rock kick. Hard to believe all the people I love listening to are in the *classic* category. Age has crept up on me—it feels like I was in my twenties just yesterday. At least the fuckers around me are getting old alongside me, so it doesn't seem quite so bad. Hell, I should feel lucky I've made it this far with some of the shit we've seen and done.

Pulling out of the compound, I hit the two-lane highway, cruising at a comfortable speed. I have a few clients on the books today, coming in for expensive pieces. They're repeat clients, so I took my time drawing up custom designs. Owning my tattoo shop has come in handy over the years, giving me the freedom I've wanted for the club and allowing me to schedule work on my time, not anyone else's. It's certainly not something that will ever make me rich, but I have everything I need in life, and the bonus is I love what I do for a living. Art has been a huge part of my life. I used to spend countless hours growing up with my nose stuck in my sketchbook, avoiding everyone else whenever possible.

Being an artist and an introvert made me an outsider to everyone else and I grew up being called a freak. Fuck them, though. They get to live their miserable lives stuck in a simple, boring box, whereas I have all the freedom a man could want. Besides, being an outcast pushed me toward tattoo apprenticing, which eventually led me to the Oath Keepers MC, so it all happened for a reason, I suppose.

The Oath Keepers became my brothers and the club my home, a place where I finally felt like I belonged and still do. I'd never trade them for anything. The brotherhood we share is a bond I'd never been privy to before I joined the MC.

Squinting, I make sure I'm not hallucinating as my eyes catch on something in the middle of the road, a lump of some sort. Whatever it is, it's big and takes up a decent portion of the road. "I swear this better not be someone trying to sabotage me. I'll shoot 'em and be done with their asses," I mutter to myself while decreasing my speed. As I ride closer to the obstruction, I'm able to make out that its a person laid out in the middle of the goddamn highway—no bullshitting.

What the fuck are they thinking?

If this is some teen being an idiot, I'm going to kick their ass into next week for pulling a life-threatening stunt like this.

I don't care how shitty life gets, don't try to kill yourself. Get your ass up and leave. Make a change and save yourself. Realize you have value and deserve to live a productive life. I dealt with my own demons growing up, with few friends and all the name-calling, but I made myself fight through the shit.

My bike crawls to a stop on the side of the road a few feet away from the stranger stretched out on the freezing asphalt. "The fuck is going on here? You better not be dead," I grumble, toeing my kickstand down and climbing off. If the long hair and big ass are any indications, I'd say it's a female with some killer curves. I shouldn't be paying attention to those things right now, but I can't help it—I'm a man, and we're visual creatures.

"Heya, sweetheart. You okay?" I approach slowly, attempting not to scare her if she's hurt. Something's got to be up. You don't just randomly lie down to nap in the middle of the flipping road. Bitches are crazy at times, but they aren't stupid. I'm surrounded by wild, intelligent women at the club, and they show us our asses quite frequently. We've grown used to it, so we expect it from time to time. The ol' ladies are sassy as hell, but we wouldn't trade any of them for the world.

"Darlin', it's okay. I'm here to help. Won't hurt you, I promise. I'm coming closer, don't be scared." I'm covered in tattoos, have a mohawk shaped into four long points, and different-colored irises—one purple from some freak mess-up with my genes. According to my mom, it's an anomaly, but to me, it just wigs people out. Sure, I get the occasional chick who says it's sexy and wants to fuck me, but it never pans out to anything solid. At six foot three and intimidating to common folks, I'm mere fuck-boy material. I am not the bring-me-home-to-the-parents type, and I've learned to accept as much.

"Ma'am?" I ask, walking around the front of her after checking both directions for vehicles. Luckily, this road isn't generally too busy. Her eyes are closed, and she's pale, so I crouch down. Her chest moves, thank fuck, so she's not dead as I'd feared. Carefully shaking her shoulder, I ask, "Hey, honey, you all right?" She still doesn't stir and I have no choice but to shift her to the shoulder of the road over by my bike and call a medic. I'd hit 2 Piece up for help and have him bring his med kit, but he's on a run. My hands move under her body, lifting and cradling her to my chest—she's cold, colder than I am. Laying her on the dead grass, I grab the small throw blanket out of my saddlebag and bundle her up in it the best I can. I don't like her lying on the cold ground like she is, so I sit beside her, adjusting her so her head's in my lap.

11

One thing's for certain—this woman is hella pregnant, and being passed out in the middle of the road seriously worries me. Grabbing my cell, I dial the local hospital and let them know I need an ambulance and where we're at, then stuff my phone away to stare at the woman in my lap.

The hospital said the ambulance will be here in a few minutes, but somehow it feels like it'll take a lifetime. I'm worried she won't make it if they don't get here soon, but there's nothing I can do to change the situation. My hands move to her arms, rubbing to bring them warmth. After a beat, I gently rest my palms on her round pregnant belly. I don't know what pushes me to do so. I've never been one to touch a woman's pregnant stomach, but with her, I can't seem to help myself.

"You okay in there, little one?" I ask, keeping my voice low and carefully smoothing my hands across her stomach. I move them back and forth, hoping her innocent child's heart is still beating.

A shift from inside makes me pause, and I am stunned at what I'm feeling. Her baby just moved. *It's alive! Oh, thank God!* "Hey there. Glad you're okay. I'm here to help. I'll take care of your momma until the medics get here, I promise." Leaving one hand on the middle of her stomach, I spread my tattooed fingers wide to keep contact with the unborn baby, offering it some semblance of comfort, hopefully. I glance at my watch, noting it's already been four minutes since I called for an ambulance. They need to hurry. I don't care where they come from, so long as someone can help this poor woman.

My other hand reaches for her hair, tucking her walnut-colored locks behind her ear and out of her face. Taking her features in closely for the first time, I notice just how breathtaking she truly is. And broken too, if the discolored bruise marring her face is any indication as to what she deals with. Her skin's pale for her tanned complexion. She's mixed heritage, but I have no idea what exactly. Trailing my fingers through her hair, I whisper, "What happened to you?" Stupid question, but my curiosity has my mind spinning. I

12

should text the brothers and let them know I didn't get far from the compound, but I can't bring myself to stop holding and caring for her. She needs me, and I'm not ready to let her go just yet.

"I'm Casey, or Spin. You can call me whatever you want, so long as you shake out of this and show me your pretty eyes. The baby's fine. I felt it move, so you just concentrate on waking up and not stressing too much. You don't have to worry about a thing. I got you. Just ask my younger sister, Mercy Mae. I won't let anything bad happen, especially to a woman. I'm not cool with that."

She's not responding at all, and who knows if she can hear me. If there's a chance, I want to put her mind at ease. Checking my watch again, it says six minutes have passed. A short amount of time under normal circumstances, but it feels like an hour in this case. It's crazy how time can either slow down or speed up when you're worried about something important.

It's silent out here in the middle of nowhere between the clubhouse and the next town, aside from me talking aloud and a few random birds making noises. Although there aren't as many birds as usual because it's winter. Just thinking of that word makes me shiver with the miserable chill. I wasn't made for the cold, that's for damn sure. "I'm not typically much of a talker. It's usually the other way around. I tattoo people and they talk my fucking ears off. Oops, sorry for cussing. I'm sure the baby doesn't need to hear it. Anyway, as I was saying, it's people jabbering on and on or asking me a million questions. They're paying me, so I can't exactly tell them Google's their friend and to use it, you know?"

Sighing, I shake my head and place my palm on her forehead. I have no idea what I'm doing, but I feel like it may be appropriate. She's cool to the touch. I'm not sure if it's a good thing or a bad thing, and this ambulance is taking forever to get here. The baby kicks my hand again, reassuring me they're both hanging on. Flicking my gaze up to the cloudy, gloomy sky, I murmur a quick thank-you that the baby is still responding to me.

"You hold on, Little Momma. Help is on the way, and I'm not leaving you in the meantime. Snuggle up to me and get warm. My big body should be good for blocking out some of the cold. You're not from around here, are you?" I'd recognize her face in a heartbeat if she was, and so would my brothers. She's the type of beauty you see and never forget. The kind of woman you'd move mountains for. *So what in the fuck is she doing with a mark on her face?*

My watch says it's been eight minutes. I should've called one of the brothers to come get us. I could've loaded her up and had them take my bike while I hauled ass to the emergency room. *Why didn't I think of that when I found her? There's no way I'd make it there before they arrive now, but still, hurry the hell up already.* I inhale deeply, then exhale my silent panic and collect myself. There's no use in both of us being out of it. One of us has to have their shit together, and it's definitely not her right now.

Finally, the faint sound of sirens fills the air, and I have a bit more hope. "See, they're almost here. They'll take good care of you. You'll get better, pop out a healthy baby, then stop by my shop sometime so I can lay eyes on you both. I'll even tattoo a sweet little footprint or handprint on you somewhere with the baby's name." She'd probably take one look at me and turn in the opposite direction. Too bad because she's someone I'd certainly like to see more of. There's no ring on her finger or any significant jewelry I can find, so who knows? She may be single. If she wasn't before, hopefully she is now after the injury on her face.

I'll never understand how a man can hit a woman. I don't care how angry you are—you protect them, not hurt them. It's been ten minutes, and I can't stop staring at her. *I feel like I know her, yet she hasn't said one word.* Ten minutes on the side of the road, holding someone while simultaneously praying they'll be okay, is both the longest and shortest time you have with them. She may not have said anything to me, but it's long enough for me to meet her baby and to notice all the tiny freckles she has in random spots. There's even one near the top corner of her lip. It's ridiculously sexy, but I'm not trying to go there right now.

The sirens become louder, the ambulance is finally close enough for me to see it and watch as it speeds down the road toward us. The baby starts shifting around again, and I lightly rub. "Don't worry. They're here to help your momma. It'll be noisy for a while, but then it'll calm down again, and you can rest." I'd stand to greet the EMTs, but I don't want to jostle the woman or make her lose any of the heat I've been able to give her.

Both guys quickly jump out, waving. I know them both, one better than the other, from when my brothers have been hurt. Usually, 2 Piece fixes us all up, but on occasion, we have to call an ambulance or go straight to the local clinic for help.

"Spin, what's up, man?" the medic greets, and I nod. He grabs his bag and comes toward us while putting on his latex gloves. The other guy roots around in the back of the vehicle, getting the stretcher ready.

"Hey, thanks for coming."

"Does she have a latex allergy?" he begins as soon as he's close enough not to yell and continues to pepper questions. "Was she with you? Did she pass out riding?"

Shaking my head, I bite down on my lip, uneasy about the fact that I don't know how she ended up out here or how long she's been like this. "Nah, I found her. She was lying in the middle of the road, unconscious. I pulled her to the side and wrapped her in my blanket to try and warm her up."

"Do you know anything about her? Name, age, where she lives?"

"Nothing. I've never seen her before," I reply bluntly, wishing I did know something about her to share.

"Nothing? You have a penchant for saving women, huh?"

The last woman I helped, I thought she was "the one," but she wasn't. Saved her from a shitty situation, but I was too late. She ended up needing to be admitted to a psych ward for an evaluation

15

and never came back out. Life fucked her world up pretty damn good.

"Look, man, the only thing I know is it took you guys ten minutes to get here, and they were probably the longest ten minutes of my fucking life." I grumble, then wince. *Shit.* "Sorry for cussing, little baby." I rub her pregnant belly again, catching a quizzical look from the medic.

Shrugging, I rationalize. "The baby doesn't need to hear the cussing."

He lifts his brows in surprise, but then nods, going about checking the woman over. "This your baby?"

"No, I don't know her," I repeat, thinking he's starting to test me. He must not believe this was all a chance encounter.

"Did you check her stomach?"

"No, I didn't look at her like that. I glanced her over quickly to make sure she wasn't bleeding and didn't have any bones sticking out in places, but nothing else."

"I'd say she's six months or so. You want to be a daddy?"

I roll my eyes. If I hadn't met him a couple of times in the past, I might be offended, but he's good people and is only doing his job. I mean, he must be if he's saving people every day. I'm simply a random dude in the wrong place at the right time kind of guy, I reckon.

"What were you doing when you found her?" He gently probes around her neck for a beat before instructing, "Carefully hold her head still while I place her in a collar. I don't think she has a neck injury, but you can never be completely sure."

Fuck. I hope I didn't injure her more by hauling her up into my lap to keep her warm.

16

Doing as he says, I release her once the brace is in place and then help as much as I can to get her on a long flat board. Then I answer his question, "I was on my bike, headed for my shop."

He continues, making me want to punch him. "And she was just lying there, no movement?"

He running for the sheriff spot or something I don't know about? Christ. "Nothing. Sprawled out in the middle of the road."

Both guys get the straps in position over her body, then lift and place her on a stretcher. "She's cold. She'll need blankets," I mutter, covering her in mine again and tucking it around her legs to keep the warmth in.

"You did good, man. Thanks for staying with her and calling us."

"Of course. Do you know what's wrong with her?"

"Not yet, but we'll get an IV in her and go from there. Poor woman. She's got a few bumps on her, but I'm thinking they're from her fall."

"You believe she tripped?"

He shakes his head. "No, I think she passed out cold and got banged up a bit when she hit the ground. She should wake up soon with fluids and rest."

"How can you tell?" I watch as they load her into the back of the ambulance, wishing I could ride with her.

"When you've been at this as long as we have, you get a sense about these things and what will happen."

"All right. Which hospital are you headed to? I'll follow."

"She'll get a room at St. David's. You don't have to come. We can take it from here. Want to give me your number so I can let you know if she makes it?"

17

"I'll follow. I don't want her waking up alone and freaked out," I respond as he heads for the driver's side.

"Then you better become family, and fast."

"I am. I'm going to be her husband." I head for my bike after he flashes me an amused grin. *I promised them both I'd make sure they get the care they need, and I'm seeing to it.*

Grabbing my cell, I quickly shoot off a text to my appointments and let them know I'll reschedule with them later today. I'll hang out for a bit at the hospital to check on the woman and also in case the actual sheriff has any questions that I won't be able to answer.

CHAPTER TWO

Naomi

Twenty-four Hours Earlier...

There's no other choice.

I have to get away.

I've been waiting for the right opportunity, and this is it, I think as I eagerly watch my ex—Jack—reverse out of the parking spot and then leave the tiny apartment complex. He'll be back, though. It's been non-stop from him, not accepting our break-up. If I stay here and don't take Jack back, I'm afraid his father may end up killing me. I moved out and got this place to be in my own space, but of course, it didn't pan out as planned.

I've been researching ever since his father, Tommy, threatened me. There's a ton of places that will help a woman if she needs it, but none of them offer real protection. They may say they have a police presence or anonymous facilities, but I know none of them could keep Tommy from finding me if he desires, and he's already promised he will if I attempt to take his grandchild away from his son.

Except one. They offer safety.

Well, it's not really a shelter or whatever, but more of a "safe refuge," according to the internet. The website says they only accept a few women per year, and it was founded by a woman named Sadie. According to the About Me section, she was once pregnant and escaping from a violent man. She drove across a few states to show up at a biker compound, looking for help, and they protected her. Since then, she's married one of the officers of the motorcycle club, had another baby with him, and has founded Sadie Baby's Haven for Pregnant Women.

Unfortunately, I don't exactly have time on my side to call or email and formally ask if they'll take me in. At this point, though, what can it hurt to just show up and ask? Even beg, if necessary. If they turn me away, at least I'll be in another state, and hopefully, the distance will make it harder to find me. I doubt it, but a girl can hope, right?

Rushing to my room, I grab the small duffle bag I've had forever and toss some of my belongings inside. I don't have a roller suitcase, so I'll have to keep this one fairly light. I'm too far along in my pregnancy to be carrying heavy stuff. I cannot afford a trip to a doctor's office right now, and the last thing I need is for my name to show up anywhere.

Taking the cash I saved, I hightail it to my vehicle and hop in. I wouldn't be surprised if my car has a tracker on it or if I'm being watched. The only thing I can do is haul ass to the bus station, buy a ticket for the first one leaving, then switch it up along the way to get to Sadie's Haven. I've never had to run from someone before, so I'm new to this, but I think my plan sounds all right so far. It's better than no plan at all, anyway.

Everything goes off without a hitch, aside from me panicking every moment of the way. I know it's not healthy for my baby or me to be under so much stress, but I don't have much of a choice at this point. I'm going to trade a bit of discomfort and worry for a better future. Besides, things will be better once I make it to Texas.

Illinois is blistering cold this week, being so close to Christmas, but I try not to pay it much mind as I load up on the bus and snuggle into my coat. I should've grabbed a blanket or something, but since I was rushing, I have virtually nothing for the entire trip south. The bus will heat up, I'm sure, once it gets going. It's packed full of holiday travelers all bundled up and excited to get wherever they're going. It should be warm in Texas, right? I'd google it, but I ditched my cell phone out the window on the drive to the bus station. I'll have to pick up a prepaid cell on my way wherever we end up stopping. Hopefully, they make plenty of bathroom breaks because this baby has me peeing all the time and craving crazy stuff to eat.

Digging out my book *What to Expect When You're Expecting*, I find my placeholder and snuggle in for the long drive. I have nothing but time and plenty to learn about when it comes to babies.

Eventually at some point, I doze off.

***

I'm shaken awake by a parking lot full of holes. *Ugh, bumps when you're pregnant and stuck sitting aren't enjoyable in the least bit. More like a pain in the ass, literally.* I go pee, find a prepaid cell, a bedazzled ballcap to twist my hair up and under, and a bag of salty chips that'll surely make my ankles swell by the time I reach the bottom of the bag.

Climbing back on the bus, I discover we're in Joplin, just about to cross over into Oklahoma. We have two stops in Oklahoma, then another three in Texas before getting to where I need to be, and it's going to take forever to arrive, it seems. I've never been to these states before and seeing that it's night outside, I doubt I'll remember much of it later. I can't help but be paranoid and take in all the faces I pass, as well as the various cars parked around us. Every vehicle that turns in, I watch like a hawk, but thankfully, none of them are familiar. I need to blend in with everyone else and disappear quietly into the world for this plan of mine to work successfully.

I don't know for certain if Jack's father will follow me now or eventually hunt me down, but I'm too frightened to take the chance on either. I always thought he was a nice guy. A little rough around the edges at times, but respectful to me.

Boy did he have me fooled.

21

But then again, so did Jack.

Our relationship wasn't going well, to put it lightly, so I thought to spare us both the trouble, I'd move out, and he could pop around to see the baby on occasion once it's born. I must've had my blinders on because the moment I let Tommy into my apartment, a switch was flicked. I'll never forget the stunned look on his face that quickly morphed into anger when I told him I didn't love his son or want to be with him. His hand struck out in a flash, and then I was on the floor, clutching my face and crying out in pain.

He'd hit me.

I've never been abused by a man before, and I always swore to myself I'd never stick around if it ever happened. I know it is hard to leave, and it's scary to possibly experience more abuse, but the only way it'll change is if I do something about it. I have to think of my baby and their future as well as my own. I refuse to allow Tommy to make me his punching bag, and who knows if Jack will end up the same way. I'm not taking any chances, and I refuse to feel guilty for leaving with the baby.

Fuck both of those guys. They deserve nothing from me at this point, and that's exactly what they'll receive.

Being patient enough to wait to leave and then getting up the nerve to actually take the leap has been the toughest decision out of this process so far. Having to pretend to Jack when he's come around that I'm okay and not going to do anything stupid. *His words, not mine.* Today, he'd stopped over and told me he was planning to move into my new place and allowing the other to go without paying the remaining rent. My teeth had grit together while he had told me his plan, and I was forced to pretend to be accepting of the shitty, irresponsible prospect. I could have fought him on it, but what would've been the point? I've been pushing him away and telling him it's over for the past two weeks, yet he hasn't listened. In it all, I've realized I don't love him, and I never truly have. My feelings were surface-level, right on top to keep me blinded enough, but no more.

I'm awake now, and again, fuck that guy.

Pulling my book back out, I attempt to read and block out all the thoughts, but it doesn't work. Thankfully, pregnancy fog takes over, and I end up passed out.

***

The next time I wake, we're stopped and unloading. I picked a tiny town called Salado to end my bus ride, and it looks like the perfect spot, full of no one I know and friendly smiles as I pass each person.

Sadie's Haven is supposed to be around this area somewhere, along with a motorcycle club, from what I gathered, but I don't have any idea where they are exactly. They don't put addresses on their website, and due to the safety issue, I understand their reasoning. It's why you have to email them or call ahead to set everything up. Even then, the site says you'll be picked up at another location completely before being allowed to see the actual place you'll be staying. It seems well thought out and organized, which I have a great appreciation for.

Doubtful there's a public library to use the internet here, so I'll have to ask around. The trouble is, who do I trust? Anyone could give me the wrong address to be a jerk or kidnap me. I've read all kinds of stories about the border problems down here, and being a curvy pregnant lady alone won't work in my favor. One guy could bop me over the head while another shoves me in the back of a car, and then I'd be toast. Lost in the corrupted trade for possibly the rest of my life. I'd rather keep to myself, stay alert, and not be kidnapped or beaten. *No thanks.*

My feet take me to a small burger place. It's a tiny hole-in-the-wall type restaurant, but the smells coming from inside have my tummy growling. "All right, tiny baby of mine, you'll get a burger,

23

but no fries and only water. We need to save money," I mutter to my belly as I pat it and walk inside. There are colored Christmas lights draped around and a tiny Christmas tree on the counter, making it a bit festive and reminding me it's literally days until Christmas. "Maybe a milkshake, but only if it's chocolate," I reason as an elderly couple flash me a friendly smile. *What is it with Texans smiling at everyone? Are they all like this?* I grin in return, not wanting to be an asshole, and mosey my way on up to the counter.

"Can I help you, ma'am?" a young woman asks, then blows a bubble with her gum.

Charming. Hope she doesn't do that while making my shake.

"Hi. I'll have whatever smells so amazing back there and a chocolate shake, please. Size small."

"The cook was making a Dirty South. And this early? You know it's breakfast time?"

"Excuse me?" I crave all things at all hours of the day. This baby does not discriminate whatsoever.

"The burger you want is called the Dirty South Burger."

"Okay. I'll take one."

"Anything else?"

"Yes. Do you know of a biker club around here or Sadie's Haven?"

She shoots me an incredulous look, her brow raising. "Ma'am, do you have any idea where you are? There's bikers *everywhere* here."

"Right." I nod, pretending I know as much while digging through my bag to get some cash.

"I got it, sweetheart," the elderly man says as he hands the cashier his bank card.

"Oh, um… thank you. That's not necessary."

The lady by his side nods. "You save your money, honey, and spend it on a Christmas gift for the baby. Buy him something cute."

"Him?" I ask. I've given no clues away to the gender.

She grins, and her significant other chuckles. "My wife ordered the same thing for breakfast when she was pregnant, and each time, it was a boy. We've got three of them. Grown now, with their own kids."

"Oh, the grandkids are so much fun!" The woman cuts in, her eyes sparkling with the love she has for her family. She places her hand in mine, tugging me to the table they were occupying. "We couldn't help but overhear you're looking for directions. My Sam and I have lived here for forty-eight years. If anyone can tell you where to go, it's us."

"Wow, forty-eight?"

"Yep. Sam, help out this sweet young lady, would you, please?"

"Already one step ahead of you, Trish. I was getting a piece of paper." He hands us one of the cashier's empty tickets, turning it over. On the back, he's drawn me a map. "Now, you want to go back to 35, then this way a little, and you turn here. Go a ways down this road, about ten minutes past a bar on the side of the road. You'll see a few turnoffs, but you want the second one. The road will disappear between some trees. It looks like it goes nowhere, but the compound's back there. They'll stop you at the gate, so think about what you want to say when you get there."

"Thank you. Your kindness won't be forgotten."

Trish waves me off. "It's what we do here. Gotta help each other out or else what kind of world would we be living in?"

25

Nodding, the cashier brings my food. Sam hands her some tip money, squeezing her shoulder with affection. I have a feeling several of those forty-eight years have been stopping in here to share their kindness while enjoying the burgers.

"You take care of yourself, and good luck with finding your friends."

"Thank you again, and take care."

Wolfing down the burger like a starved beast, I study the map and continue to check my surroundings. I'm states away, yet still paranoid Tommy and Jack will waltz through the door and drag me back home. *No, I refuse to call that place home. It's time for a change, and as far as anyone else knows, I'm a Texan.*

The map is basically made up of a couple of scribble lines all connected and a few dots on each side to indicate the bar and Sadie's Haven. If it's so bare out there, then it can't be too hard for me to find. I have to save as much of my money as possible. I'm not sure how much it'll cost for them to take me in or if I'll be able to find a job anytime soon. Looks like the only choice I have is to walk.

Asking for a to-go cup of hot water, I grab my bag and begin my trek. It's chilly outside, and I need the water to help keep me warm. I didn't bring my heavy jacket because I thought it'd be too much, but now I'm regretting it. A cloudy morning in December and the temperature is cold enough to have me shivering. I'm sure it'll warm up as the day goes on, and I know my body will as well once I get walking for a while. Crossing the bridge over the highway with the cars speeding by is pretty damn nerve-wracking, but I make it.

Following the hand-drawn map, I walk, and walk, and walk some more. All day, to the point my entire body aches, and eventually, I don't remember falling asleep. Especially not while recklessly walking down the middle of the abandoned two-lane road.

CHAPTER THREE

Spin
Present...

The woman is finally awake, and I can't stop staring at her. I have no clue who she is, yet in the same breath, I feel like I know her far too well. The nurse brought me to her room after she told the woman how I'd found her and called an ambulance for help. Apparently, waiting around was enough for her to want to thank me.

"Purple hair and a purple eye... your favorite color or something?" she asks after a moment of taking me in. I know I can be a lot for some people. Toss in the black jeans, biker boots, fitted thermal, and my cut, and I send people in the other direction. Unless they know me—then it's a different story entirely. I may be intimidating at first impression, but I'd give you the shirt off my back if you asked nicely.

"Or something..." I've always worn a colored contact in one eye because it's blown. My iris is completely black, and it fucks with people more than the purple iris does. They can reason with a fake icy-gray eye but not a black one, for some reason. The less questions I have to deal with, the better. And don't get me started about Halloween—each year, I get so many damn questions about it being a costume. No, motherfucker, I really have a purple eye and a grayish, almost white, contact in my other eye to save you from your made-up emotional trauma.

"You're so colorful," she replies thoughtfully.

Her comment doesn't surprise me, but it still manages to burn on the inside and solidifies why I generally stay away from people. I've been called a freak since I was a little kid. All my ink came after the crazy hair colors and styles when I was thrust into my life's work. I loved to sketch when I was a teen, which eventually led me to a tattoo shop. The first needle hit my flesh at that same shop, and I knew tattooing was what I was meant to be doing.

Joining the club came along shortly after. The first brother strolled in, looking for an artist to give him some custom club ink. After a few sessions of tattooing him, I knew I needed a motorcycle as well. He had this look of freedom about him, and I desperately craved that peace with everything I had.

"You're kinda beautiful, you know that?" she continues, taking in my silence and catching me completely off guard.

No one has ever called me beautiful before.

"Yeah? So are you, Little Momma," I respond more bluntly than usual.

She quietly gasps, eyes growing wide. "Wait… you're an Oath Keeper?"

A brow raises as my back stiffens. *What's she know about my club?* "And if I am?"

Her inquisitive gaze flickers over my frame once more, this time pausing on the many different patches of my cut. Attention thrown our way is typically negative until people get to know us. Her interest has me on edge, ready to beat feet and get the fuck out of here. "I was looking for you guys?" It comes out more like a question than a statement. She's obviously unsure if it's the right answer.

She doesn't strike me as a bike bunny or a club slut, especially not pregnant, but what do I know when it comes to women? I can fuck and tattoo well. Anything past that and I don't get much feedback from them. "What's your name, doll?"

"Naomi, and you're… Spin?" She nods to my breast, where my name is sewn into the leather. The opposite side has an identical patch with my club position. I'm the treasurer and a fully patched officer. Have been for years.

"Yeah. I introduced myself to you on the side of the road."

She points to her head, cocking it. She flashes a goofy smile and mentions, "Comatose. Remember?"

"Of course. Longest ten minutes of my fucking life." I automatically cringe with my language around the baby. "My mouth is crap at times. I'm trying to mind it around your kid."

She glances around the room before her attention lands on her cute belly poking out of the covers. There's just something about pregnant bellies I find ridiculously sexy on a woman. "You're attempting not to swear because of my baby?"

Nodding, I can't help but stare as her teeth sink into her lower lip. *She's looking at me like I'm a popsicle, and she wants a lick. Or some dick. I mean both. Fuck. What is it with this chick?* "I was saying I found you and introduced myself while waiting for help. You okay?"

"I am now, thanks to you. You guys really are a *safe haven*, aren't you?"

A safe haven?

What's she talking about? Then it hits me like a ton of bricks.

This woman is in danger.

She wants Sadie's help—well, essentially the club's protection—from whatever evil's hurting her.

"He give you that nasty bruise on your face?" I ask with a chin lift toward her. I don't know anything about her story, yet I'm ready to fuck the world up on her account.

Suddenly, Naomi can no longer meet my stare as she slowly nods, her fingers plucking at the thin blanket. She has no reason to be ashamed or embarrassed. Quite the opposite. It takes a lot of strength for a woman to get out and ask for help. In her case, she would have had to drop everything, leaving whatever she may have had behind to start fresh here. Her walking down the road doesn't make sense,

29

though, and we haven't had a recent vote in church about taking in anyone new.

"Wanna tell me exactly what you were doing passed out in the middle of the road? If you came here for what I'm thinking, then someone should've picked you up to make sure you weren't followed. There's a way we do things."

"I understand if you need to turn me away." She goes on to explain how she had to leave in a rush and ride a bus for hours on end to get here and not have any way of reaching the club. Her cheap prepaid cell has no internet, so she couldn't look up the phone number on Sadie's website, and she never had the chance to email either.

This woman was walking all damn day.

Alone.

Pregnant.

In the cold.

Just to look for the club.

She's throwing me for a loop. The bravery on her part has me more interested in her than I've ever been in the past with the other pregnant women. There's only been a few we've helped so far, but Naomi is an enigma, sucking me in already.

"I'll figure something out." The strong woman tries to put on a brave face, but she's not fooling me one bit. I bet she's terrified, and believe it or not, that's completely normal. Besides, she's crazy if she thinks I'll let her go get hurt.

There's something about her—I can't explain it, but I feel like I know her. Those ten minutes with her, alone, attempting to comfort her baby while making sure she held on, did something to me. "You don't have to figure anything out, doll. I got you. Once the doc says you're straight to go, we'll pop smoke and head to the club. I'll keep you safe."

Her chin trembles as she asks, full of disbelief, "You'll do that for me? Why?"

"Of course I will. Any man who will put that on your face while you're carrying a baby, or anytime at all, doesn't deserve you."

"It was my ex's father. He's the one I think will hurt or kill me for leaving."

"It doesn't matter if it was the president of the United States. Any guy who raises his hand to a woman deserves to be put down."

"Thank you, Spin. Will everyone else be okay with me showing up, though? I understand there's a process. I just had to try my luck with showing up. I get it if they want to turn me away."

"They'll be fine with it. I'll speak to my brothers and get it sorted. In the meantime, how about you take it easy until the doc lets you go?"

"I can go now. Only need to sign my discharge papers. I already put my normal clothes back on and everything." I glance at her shirt, noting it's not the bland hospital gown, so she must be telling me the truth. I've been too distracted by her presence to pay attention to what clothes she's wearing. "They offered to let me stay overnight for observation, but I can't take the chance of hanging around here longer than necessary. They did an ultrasound, gave me some IV fluids, and checked my vitals. I'm okay now. The doctor believes the stress and exhaustion took a toll on me and caused me to faint."

Knowing her body was pushed to the point of passing out brings the caretaker in me to the surface. I basically raised my little sister, then helped out my club when we were searching for sex traffickers and their victims. Helping women is something deeply ingrained, and with Naomi, the feeling is tenfold.

"All right, I'll get you situated at the club. Then we can go from there with the supplies you need." I hold my hand out to assist her out of bed, and she places her palm in mine. She's really curvy with a perfect round belly poking out, but she still somehow manages to seem small to my tall frame. Her flesh against mine is electric, making zings of awareness shoot through my body.

After swiping her bag up off the chair, I hook it over my shoulder and keep her hand secured in mine.

"I can carry my bag." She starts to protest, but I'm not having it. The woman was just laid out in a hospital bed, for Christ's sake.

"So can I, Little Momma. I'll give it back to you once we get to the bike. I'll take it nice and slow so you can hold on. You start feeling faint, sick, hungry, or anything at all, you let me know."

"Okay."

"Bet," I mumble, satisfied with her easy nature. I know one thing's for sure, seeing her hot ass around the club will be a welcome sight. The brothers will agree, but I'm making it clear she's off-limits until she takes an interest in one of them. If she does, anyhow, but we're probably too rough and gruff for her tastes. Who knows? Women aren't my specialty.

We stop at the nurses' station all decked out in plastic sparkly garland and paper ornaments taped to everything. The staff here has always been friendly and helpful. I've seen a few movies with crazy nurses, but I've never come across one before. Naomi signs a few papers while the doc tells her to be careful and come back if anything feels off.

"You take care of her." An older red-headed nurse directs my way.

"Yes, ma'am. I got Little Momma's back. Won't let her push herself too hard again."

She offers me a grandmotherly grin and pats my bicep. "Oh, you're a strong one. No doubt you can handle it." Her face tints as she observes aloud, making the other nurses laugh.

"Come on, He-Man." Naomi squeezes the hand I'm still holding. She huffs a little, turning to leave. *She doesn't care about the nurse, does she?* I was being polite, nothing more. I stopped caring what people think of me long ago, but something scratches the back of my neck—this feeling like I hope Naomi isn't embarrassed to be seen with me.

"You good?"

With another sigh, she meets my gaze. "Yes." The word leaves her on a whisper.

"That didn't sound so convincing. Hit me with whatever you've got going through that beautiful head of yours."

"It's just… the woman was openly flirting with you… while you were holding my hand. The others were giggling and eyeing you up. It was rude, is all."

"Seriously? They were?" *Am I oblivious to this shit? 'Cause how the fuck did she notice them paying me any extra attention and I didn't? I was right there!*

"Yeah, they were all doe-eye, hanging on your every breath."

A chuckle escapes as I shake my head. "Nah, they were just being friendly. Most people around here are the same."

We walk through the electric doors into the Texas air as she casts me a suspicious glance. "Are they female?"

With a shrug, I admit, "Usually, yeah."

She grunts. "Harrumph… exactly what I thought. It's because you're hot."

My throat seems to close up on me as I absorb what she's said. *Naomi thinks I'm hot? And she believes it's the reason why women are kind to me around here?* Pausing next to my motorcycle, I remove the bag and spin Naomi around. "Changed my mind."

"Huh?" She squeaks, fear filling her expression.

"Calm down, doll. I'm talking about the bag. I'm wearing it across my chest. No way am I putting this on you to pull you back with the wind. It's too dangerous."

"Oh! But won't you be uncomfortable?"

"Don't worry about me. Keep you and the baby in mind." I gesture to her stomach, then place my hands on her thighs, fingers resting right under her voluptuous booty.

She squeals a little, her face flaming as she asks, "What are you doing?"

"Hands on my shoulders, babe. Hold on tight while I get you on my bike."

"Woah, big guy! I can get on myself. Don't worry."

"Nope. Won't have you stressing your body or the baby. The ride will be taxing enough on you."

"Don't tell me you're one of those controlling types."

"I'm not. I'd never control you in any way. I care about your safety and health, about your happiness and wellbeing."

Her lower lip trembles as tears spring in her eyes. "You're seriously sweet, you know that?" she mumbles, placing her hands on my shoulders.

"Hold on tight, Naomi."

With her nod of assurance, I tighten my grip and lift. She yells and giggles the entire time, making me grin like a damn fool. I love hearing her sound so carefree, and yet it makes me rage inside that someone had attempted to steal this brightness from her. They better hope I never come across them, or they'll learn what true darkness feels like when I rip them apart.

"Feet down." I direct and watch as she reaches with her tiptoes on either side of the bike. Spinning the duffle bag to my front, I continue to have her hold on to my arm while I carefully put my leg

34

over. Normally, I'd never get on my bike this way with someone else, but I needed to get her on it first so she didn't hurt herself. "Wrap your hands around my waist and hold on tight."

"Okay, I will."

"Promise me you won't let go until I tell you to."

"I promise, Spin. The only way I'm coming off your bike is if I fall."

Fuck.

She shouldn't say something like that. Now it has me thinking about keeping her.

CHAPTER FOUR

Naomi

Not gonna lie, I was way off when it came down to what I should expect. I had all sorts of vivid details conjured up, thinking Sons of Anarchy-type of clubhouse. Yeah, I couldn't have been more wrong—it's nothing in comparison. Spin calls it the compound, and this place definitely fits the name as it's large, taken care of, and well-protected.

We slowly ride through a gated entrance with another biker standing guard to unlock it and let us in. A tall chain-link fence from either direction matches the entrance gate and seems to span around the entire property. Spin says it's to keep people out so we're always safe. I can't help but wonder if it's to keep people inside as well. I'm trying to take it all in with a grain of salt and be open-minded, but it's a bit of culture shock.

The few half-naked women we passed while walking through the common area were quick to give me a once-over and turn away uninterested. I have a feeling if I were male, I'd have been welcomed differently. Spin assures me most of the MC members have an ol' lady, so there are no other club whores around. His words, not mine. I'd never call a woman a club whore, but again, not judging. I'm here hoping for help, not to chastise them on their club terms and way of life.

Now I'm sitting in Spin's room, minding my own business. Or at least striving to, as every bone in my body is screeching at me to get up and poke around in his stuff to find out every detail I can about him. One thing that's for certain, without me having to snoop around, is the man loves art, and I'm not talking about any old designs. First of all, one wall is dark purple, another gray, and the final two are white. His bedspread is jet black, along with his curtains and pillows. His dresser and desk are both littered with multiple sketch pads, charcoal pencils, oil paints, markers, tattoo ink, some weird-shaped rulers, white erasers, smudge sticks, and other artsy-type stuff. There are large, elaborate hand drawings in frames on the walls, a few paintings, as well as one in ink and an easel off to the side. Something tells me this is all him—his personal works of art.

He should be selling these in galleries in big cities, not locking them away. Such creations deserve to be shared with the world, which tells me there's a story behind him locking them away.

Who are you, Spin?

What's your story?

Spin told me to stay in his room until he comes to get me and gives me the "all clear" or else I'd be walking around right now, checking out the entire space. After lying in the hospital bed for hours, I want to stretch my limbs a bit and explore. And don't get me started on the ride over here. It was completely exhilarating. I can't remember the last time I felt so peaceful and free. No wonder people love motorcycles as much as they do. I didn't mention it to Spin, but that was my first time riding. I figured it might freak him out too badly to let me ride. He was already concerned with me being pregnant, so I kept my mouth shut about never having been on a motorcycle before.

I'll never forget it, or him.

A knock interrupts my thoughts, making me sit up straight. It could be anyone, as I highly doubt Spin would knock on his own bedroom door to come inside. "Uh, Spin's not here! He'll be back soon," I yell instead. Whoever it is, hopefully they'll come back later.

"It's Sadie. I want to speak with you."

"Of course! Please come in," I call through the door and watch as it opens. A tiny sprite of a woman enters, flashing a warm smile. She reminds me of a biker Tinkerbell, but I have a feeling her bite is a lot sharper than Tink's.

"Hi, I'm Sadie."

Standing, I hold my hand out. "It's nice to meet you. I'm Naomi, and I hope I didn't stir up any trouble by coming here." I plop back down on the comfy chair. I'm much bigger than her, and I don't want her to feel like I'm being overbearing by randomly showing up or from my size.

"Trouble? No way. You caught everyone off guard, but it's good to have them on their toes occasionally." She sits on the chair's arm, right next to me, gesturing to my stomach. "How far along are you?" she questions, and I feel like she's genuinely curious, not just trying to fill the silence. Finding people who truly care about strangers is hard to come by these days, and it instantly notches up my respect for her to another level.

"I'm past my six-month mark. I swear it's taking forever for my due date to get here, and this kid loves to play kickball with my bladder."

She laughs. "It'll be here before you know it, then you'll be scrambling. Trust me, I felt the same way with mine. You want them to hurry up and come out, then you miss them and wish they were still in your belly at times. Motherhood is unlike any experience I've ever had. Never thought I could love a tiny human so much when I first met them."

My smile's wide by the time she stops talking. "I can't wait for everything you just said," I admit. I'll have my own little person to shower with love and cuddles.

"So, Naomi, tell me what brought you here."

Going into the same spiel I'd shared with Spin, I tell her everything, choking up at the end. I hope I don't sound like a whiney ass who ran away from a man wanting me around. It was never like that to me, though, but rather an unhappy relationship that morphed into an even more toxic one at the end.

She nods when I finish, grabbing my hand to lightly squeeze it. I swear I can see the empathy in her eyes, and it brings me an overwhelming sense of comfort. She seems like someone who genuinely wants to help women in danger, thank God. I knew there was a chance her website could end up being fake or a front for something else. I had no idea if I'd show up and they'd sell me across the border or use my baby for some sort of twisted harvesting. Maybe lock me away as their personal sex prisoner or something else just as sick and twisted.

"We've helped a few women. Not as many as I'd like to, but it's a start."

Nodding, I eagerly hang on to each word, hoping she'll allow me to stay. "Definitely. It shows you have a big heart to extend assistance as you have."

"Thank you. Besides, it's Christmas. The brothers can't turn you away."

Holding up my crossed fingers, I murmur, "I sure hope not. I was praying the whole way here."

"Holding onto hope is the best thing now and in the future. I'm sure you know pregnancy can be hard and emotional journey. I just want you to know you're here now, and you're not alone. If you need help, even a shoulder to cry on, I'm here."

A tear escapes as my emotions well up all over again. These damn hormones have my tears all over the place lately. "First Spin, and now you. Why would you do this for me, for a person you've never met before?"

"Because at one point in my life, this was the only place I could run to. I was terrified my brother would turn me away."

"I take it he didn't?"

She shakes her head. "No. He welcomed me with open arms, and he protected me when the time came. They all did. This club took me in and gave me everything I needed when I had absolutely nothing but a clunker of a car filled with some of my clothes. They changed my life for the better, and I'll never forget it. If I can offer that for one person, let alone multiple, it's what I want to do."

We're interrupted by Spin opening the door. He offers up a pleased grin, saying, "Hey, Sadie. I see you found our girl."

Her brows jump as she flashes a swift glance between us. She quickly covers it up with a smile and says, "Sure did. I take it you talked to the boys?"

"Yeah."

"And? Good news?"

He moves to stand beside me, taking my hand in his. "Prez said Naomi can stay. We voted on it, and the brothers are on board. There's a catch, though."

"Oh?" Sadie gets to her feet, staring Spin down.

I stammer. "I-I won't be trouble. I promise."

"Don't worry, doll. It's nothing like that. The condition is the extra rooms we have at the club are already taken. We have people in town now and in the future to spend the holiday here. We don't like our friends and brothers spending them alone."

"I understand. I have a little money for a hotel, but I'm afraid it'll maybe last a week, no longer. I can work, though, if anyone needs an employee."

"I'm not putting you in some hotel, unprotected," he cuts me off. "Last thing you or the baby needs is to be scared, hungry, and alone. Not happening."

Sadie's shoulders relax. "Agreed. What's the plan then?"

"Well, if Naomi's okay with it, she'll have to share my room with me. At least until the holidays are over and a spare room opens up."

Sadie grins. "This is a wonderful idea. I'll leave you two to talk things over and get settled. Nice meeting you, Nay." She gives me a nickname right off the bat, making me feel even more welcome than she already has from our chat.

"Nice meeting you too."

We watch her leave, Spin offering her a chin lift on her way out. He drops my hand to sink down on the edge of his bed. "So, how do you feel about what my brothers said?"

My chest bubbles up with a mixture of excitement and anxiety. Not the scared kind, but rather, the eager kind.

Share a room with a hot biker who has multi-colored eyes, a crazy tall mohawk, and a body made for sin? Uh, yeah. I'm down.

I hope I can keep from jumping him in one of my pregnancy-induced brain fogs, where all I can think about is humping a stiff dick or talented tongue. At least when I was living alone for those few weeks, I could go to town on a cucumber whenever the urge struck. Just thinking of it has me turned on.

"I don't mind sharing. A room with you, or bed, whatever. You know what I mean," I reply, feeling flustered.

Spin smirks. "It's settled then. This will be your new home, and I'll protect you and the baby. You won't have to worry about anything."

All I can think about at the moment is him on that bed. *I wonder if he sleeps naked.* My breathing becomes labored as I picture him taking his clothes off and climbing into bed each night. He clears his throat and glances down, staring at my chest a beat. His cheeks flush as he draws in a swift breath and licks his lips. My nipples are overstimulated, as each breath I take has my thin lacy bra scratching against them.

41

He stands suddenly, and I follow suit, bringing our bodies ridiculously close together. "Thank you," I manage to murmur in a daze as I take in his presence. He seems turned on, and it's only driving me even wilder. *How can I be in tune with a man I've barely met?* It seems like we have this unexplainable magnetic connection, which is throwing me off-kilter. I don't know how I'm supposed to act around him when I can't stop thinking about how badly I want to touch him and have his hands on me in return. Freaking pregnancy hormones are messing me up.

"Of course," Spin rasps and licks his bottom lip again. He clears his throat. "Excuse me." He rushes off to the bathroom, swiftly closing the door and leaving me puzzled over his quick exit.

Heaving a sigh, I happen to glance down, and right there for everyone to see are two wet spots on my chest. He got me flustered to the point I began to lactate, and it must have turned him on.

He damn sure wasn't staring at me with disgust.

So maybe, just maybe… he likes me too.

CHAPTER FIVE

Spin

I'm ashamed of myself. I got caught up in Naomi's beauty, and then when her breasts began to leak, I was in a complete trance. I ran to the bathroom to not further embarrass myself with the tent in my pants. I'm not sure what it is about her exactly to get me so damn turned on. She probably thinks I'm some creep she has to share a room with. I never meant for it to be this way. It sort of fell in my lap, and I scooped the opportunity up with both hands.

When I was in church with the brothers and they brought up the possibility of others visiting for the holidays, I immediately volunteered my room. I even vouched and pledged my protection for her. *Over eager?* Maybe.

So far, every woman Sadie has brought in, we've had one brother assigned to help maintain her safety, and the rest of us acted as backup. My volunteering didn't seem out of the ordinary to anyone at the table, but they haven't seen how curvy and gorgeous she is yet, either. I'm sure I'll catch some hell once they realize as much, but it won't bother me any.

Maybe I should offer to sleep on the couch in the rec room tonight to give her some space. She was napping in my room when I finally peeled the bathroom door open and peeked my head through like a giant chicken shit. Once I saw her eyes closed and heard the adorable soft snores leaving her lips, I ducked for cover and got the hell out of dodge. Now I have guilt clawing up my back at leaving her in there alone when she doesn't know a soul here aside from me and the brief encounter she's had with Sadie.

"You straight, bro?" Cain, our VP, asks as he slides onto the stool beside me. I may be posted up at the bar, but I'm not tossing them back. I have a beer and a glass of water resting on the bar before me, both getting warm as I mentally chastise myself and overthink things. One bed seemed like a dream come true earlier, but after getting a hard-on by her breasts alone, I'm not so sure if it's smart anymore. The other problem with not sleeping in the same bed is, if one of the visiting brothers attempts to get her in theirs, I won't be able to keep my mouth shut, and it'll be an issue for sure.

With a shrug, I watch the condensation run down the side of my water glass. The heat's cranked up in the clubhouse because none of these assholes like wearing shirts, even in the wintertime. I'm not exactly sure what to say in return.

Am I okay? I'm fine. Just disappointed in myself when I wanted to make a decent impression. Is that such a bad thing? To want to come off as a good guy to a pretty woman in a rough situation. She needs protection and trust, which I was hoping to give her both.

Peppermint, Brently's ol' lady, ducks behind the bar. She grabs a few beers and smiles warmly at Cain and me before she returns to Brently, offering him one of the bottles and sliding onto his lap. They started a bit shaky. The brother followed her home and took the door off her hinges to get her to talk to him. They've been glued at the hip ever since. Maybe I should take a page from his book and dive in head first, but who knows if it's truly the right answer in this situation. I don't want to come off as too pushy.

"Spin, talk to me." His brow shoots up, beefy-as-fuck arms crossing over his chest. He's been a fighter for as long as I've known him. He made a lot of money fighting in other clubs but has slowed down. Becoming vice president and popping out a few kids takes up the majority of his time now. He sips his protein shake, eyeing me up, looking like the intimidating motherfucker I know he can be. He's not going to let me walk away without getting something out of me. I should expect nothing less, though. This is what family is all about—the Oath Keepers have taught me as much time and again.

Sighing, I run my finger over the label on my beer. After a beat of contemplation, I admit, "I may be a bit hard up for Naomi."

"Naomi... you mean the new chick we're protecting? From the vote earlier?"

With a nod, I divulge my thoughts. "Finding her like I did... it changed something inside of me. I can't stop thinking of Naomi and wanting to be good enough for her. I don't know why or what the fuck happened, just that it did, and it has my fucking head spinning."

He emits a low whistle, lips tipping into a smirk. "Good for you, brother. And what the fuck do you mean *good enough*? You're one of the coolest dudes around here with no drama, no bad attitude, and you've been steady for as long as I've been a member. You own your own business, and I've never seen you disrespect a woman... so clue me in, 'cause she should be gone for you too."

Prez comes strolling up beside us, catching the last tidbit of Cain's spiel. His brows skyrocket as well, making me roll my eyes. They're my brothers, and by extension, nosey as hell. We're all up in each other's business at the club because we're close. We've been in more than one too many shitty situations in the past not to have each other's backs at this point.

"Ares," Cain acknowledges.

"Prez," I state, nodding my respect to the human tank. I'm not exaggerating. When it comes to massive dudes, Ares is one to head up the pack and is hella intimidating being our prez.

"The fuck you two gossiping about?"

"Nothing," I mutter.

At the same time, Cain responds, "He likes the new woman. Our brother is sprung already."

"Fuck." With a curse, my hand goes for my beer and I take a swig, attempting to wash my embarrassment down. They probably

45

think I'm trying to save another chick and don't know what I really want. I'm not captain save-a-hoe or anything. I just come across women in distress on occasion and jump in to help them if needed. There are worse habits to have.

"Hmm…" He grunts, resting his bear-sized hands on his hips, taking me in. "You like her? Enough to keep her?"

I give him a jerky nod as 2 Piece waltzes behind the bar flashing his ol' man a grin. His ol' lady is around here somewhere as well. 2 Piece, Ares, and Avery have been solely committed to each other for years—a real live threesome, front and center. I envy their level of love and commitment and am glad the club is open-minded enough to accept their type of love.

"Stop stressing about whatever has you stuck in your head and tell her."

"Ah… she just got here, Prez."

Cain butts in. "True. You don't want to scare her away. Maybe go easy for a little while and not jump straight to giving her whiplash."

Prez huffs, grumbling to himself. He obviously disagrees with the VP and won't hesitate to say what's on his mind. "Wasting time is all it is. Trust me. I pissed away far too much time holding on to unspoken feelings. Worst mistake I ever made. Don't wait too long, so she's already gone when you're ready to spill how you feel." Prez is fucking crazy. A madman who chops up the bodies of his enemies and feeds them to the pigs at the farm, yet the brother is giving me advice on love. I guess if anyone can be the poster child of love having no bounds, it'd be him.

"I don't even know her. I found her on the side of the road… we briefly talked in the hospital and then again earlier. I'm so fucking confused. This chick has me in knots over wanting her already, 'cause it's too soon for this to be happening."

"But you felt a connection?" 2 Piece questions, suddenly neck-deep in the conversation I didn't want to have. *Bunch of nosey fuckers.*

"Unlike I've ever had before," I confess, feeling my shoulders lighten by saying it aloud. It's out in the open now and can't be taken back. I have to own it, and I intend to.

Cain bops his head, not bashful for a second to point out when he's right about something. "See. I knew it." It takes everything in me not to flip him off. *Cocky fucker.*

Ares gestures to 2 Piece, stepping off to the side so they can speak quietly while I shoot daggers at my nearly full beer. I don't intend on finishing it. I don't know why I ordered it in the first place. Probably habit of sitting at the bar. I shouldn't be drinking with a guest and a baby on the way. It doesn't taste good today anyhow.

"I've always caught shit for how I look." I finally acknowledge my deep secret I've kept locked tightly away, my words quiet enough not to be overheard by anyone else.

"I never thought you gave a fuck."

"I didn't. Not really, anyhow." I shake my head, rubbing my palms over my black-wash jeans to get the sudden itch out of them.

"But you care now? Enough to let it bother you?"

"She's about to have a baby. I want to be a good example."

"Fuck, bro."

"What?"

"You're gonna patch this chick. I can see it already. You'll marry her and put a property patch on her." I stare at him, silent. He continues, "Wouldn't be the first time a woman rolled up in here with a baby on the way from another and was claimed by one of us. Look at Twist and Sadie. Brother was gone, straight mental, and she managed to bring him back from the deep end. I thought the brother

47

was going to kill himself, but then he found his ol' lady. They've been together for years, and I don't see Twist ever letting her go."

"She was exactly what he needed, then and now. Helped heal his soul from losing his child."

Cain concurs, reaching for my beer I've been glaring at. I wave it off, giving him permission to drink the barely touched beverage. I'd have wasted it anyhow. "You think Naomi could be the one for me? I'm not as jaded as Twist was, but I have my hang-ups I deal with too."

I'm self-conscious, an over-thinker, and protective of my baby sister to probably an unhealthy level. In my defense, she's tiny. Then again, I'm overly protective of all vulnerable women. Someone has to be. My mother was murdered, and it fucked up my sister, Mercy Mae, to the point she nearly took a dive off a building at a young age. Mercy never spoke about it after she grieved, and at the time, I was too young to know what to do with my sister. She grew up here and in the tattoo shop. With the brothers' help and the old prez, she turned out whole and healthy. She isn't perfect, but none of the best ones are.

If only I could remember the sentiment when it comes to myself.

"If you're torn up over her and this is only day one? Fuck yes, I think she is." His eyes grow wide. "Speaking of… you didn't tell us she's a knockout. And do not repeat that shit around my ol' lady or I'll be missing one of my nuts by mornin'." I try to hold back my chuckle from escaping, but it's no use.

London is crazy enough she'd fuck him up some way or another. Maybe not saw a nut off since she seems to enjoy popping out a ton of Cain's babies, but she'd mess with him somehow. Probably drop his car off at the chop shop or send it off the side of a cliff and call it a day, or at minimum go joyriding again and burn through the expensive wide tires while scraping the rims against a curb. Just thinking of the possibilities gives me the shivers and makes my asshole pucker.

Glancing at Naomi, her face is lit up at me laughing. She flashes a wide smile in my direction, and the air in my chest stutters to the point I feel like I can't breathe. *How can she do this to me with a mere smile? Is this really how fast things happen when you meet your soulmate?*

What am I saying? I'm getting ahead of myself, and I need to pump the breaks a bit. Take it easy, one baby step at a time so I don't send her running for the hills. It's going to be hard, though. I want to wrap her up and stick her in my pocket so I can carry her with me everywhere. That shit sounds strange, yet it also makes perfectly good sense in my mind.

As soon as she's close enough, I greet her. "Hey, Little Momma. How you doin'?"

"I'm okay. I must've passed out on you." Her eyes are full of questions, but I can't give her any answers right now because the last thing I want to do is embarrass her in any way with my truth.

Nodding, I slowly grab her hand, giving her the opportunity to deny me if she wishes. "You had one helluva day, and it's late. You deserve to rest and get your strength back. By the way, this is the vice president of the club, Cain." I meet his gaze. "This is my Naomi." The word slips in unplanned, labeling her as mine in front of club members. Not good unless I plan to formally claim and patch her as Cain had taunted me with moments before.

"Hi. Nice to meet you, Cain. I appreciate you letting me stay here."

He grins. "You too, Naomi. Not a problem at all. Stick close to Spin so he can protect you if needed. Though I don't see anything happening to you while you're here. They'd be stupid to show up trying to hurt a woman in this clubhouse. Those are the types we show *special* lessons to."

49

"If only that worked online too. I am scared to check my accounts. I'm sure he's drug my name through the dirt. You know how people believe everything they see online, no matter how untrue it may be." She frowns, making every beat of my heart want to make her smile again.

"Cyberstalking is disgusting. Done by cowards. Don't give them a second thought. Anyone with half a brain knows better than to believe the bullshit those narcissists spiel. As far as I see it, if they can't provide legit proof, then they're nothing but liars," Cain says.

Her fingers tremble on the hand I'm not holding before she clenches it into a fist, hiding her anxiousness. I'd never have noticed had I not been checking her over when I caught it. "He's right." I grumble. "Fuck stalkers and cyberbullies. Bunch of pansies I'd gladly teach a lesson to. Real men don't act like that. You don't worry about anything. You have me, remember?"

Her teeth sink into her lower lip as she meets my concerned stare. "I remember. Thank you so much, Spin."

With a wave of my hand, I change the subject, wanting to put her at ease. "You hungry? How's the baby?" Her stomach growls loudly, and the three of us burst into laughter. Her cheeks flush, so I give her hand a soft squeeze. She has no reason to be bashful around me. I held her in my arms on the side of the road. There's no more vulnerable time that I can think of with someone than being unconscious in their care. "You're still looking like you need more sleep, and the doctor said to take it easy, especially over the next few days. Want me to grab something to eat and bring it to the room? You can lie in bed and prop your feet up?"

Cain slaps me on my shoulder, obviously pleased with my suggestion. He has a house full of kids, so he'd know the best way to take care of a pregnant chick. I'm glad because I know next to nothing and only want to make Naomi's life easier. She's already been through a tough enough time, and she needs to realize it comes to an end with me.

"Yum, sounds great. I haven't eaten since this morning, aside from the IV and Jell-O at the hospital. Oh, and nothing with onions. They make me puke. Sometimes the smell alone will set me off. It sucks."

"No pukey onions. Got it. I'm glad because I think they're gross and should only be used as a form of torture."

Naomi laughs. "Have a good night, Cain. And I'll see you shortly." She winks at me, and I nearly combust on the spot from wanting her so badly. I'm left watching her every step, the sway of her hips putting me in a hypnotic trance.

"You're hooked and in trouble if you don't lock it down soon," he states as soon as she's out of earshot. "If it were me, it'd already be done."

"Huh?" I'm drawn out of my staring contest with Naomi's big round ass. *More cushion for the pushin'.*

He chuckles, downing the rest of the beer. "Nothing, man. Forget it. Go take your woman some food, and tomorrow, grab her a body pillow, a massager, and some sweet snacks. Nothing salty. It'll make her swell up and be in pain. Make sure she drinks plenty of water, and she'll probably want chocolate milk for heartburn."

"Wow. Okay. I'll text you. I'm sure I'll have more questions."

He stands to leave. "You're going to knock her up after she has that kid. I can already tell. One taste of pregnancy won't be enough for you, will it?"

Shaking my head, I quietly admit what had crossed my mind earlier. "I think I'm obsessed with her pregnant body and everything else about her."

"Welcome to the club, bro. My ol' lady owns my ass, hook, line, and sinker. I'll catch you later. One beer is my limit as London's waiting in my bed."

"Ride easy, brother." I punctuate it with a fist bump and head for the kitchen.

CHAPTER SIX

Spin

I'm awoken from a delicious-sounding moan and sweet, sweet grinding on my stiff cock. *Fuck. I must be dreaming again. This is too good to be true.* Soft lips meet mine when a groan escapes me, my hands moving to Naomi's wide hips and griping them tightly. *Double fuck. I want inside her.*

She pulls away, one hand shifting behind my head to tilt it while her other hand grips my jaw. Her breast is placed to my mouth and she moans. "Suck it." They're wet, leaking again, and I'm ready to come in my boxers for a third time in twenty-four hours. Doing as I'm told, my tongue eagerly laps at her hard nipple, stroking the point and tasting her. I've never had a lactating fetish before, but she's brought something new out in me, and I swear she craves it as badly as I do.

How can this woman I've barely met have such an effect on me? She was already the star in my dreams tonight, as well as my thoughts all day, and now this? I'm in heaven.

My lips latch onto her breast, drawing deeply enough to pull her milk into my mouth. The sensation has her body vibrating as she moans louder. Her pussy continues to slide up and down my long shaft, my vision flickering with bright flashes of bliss. She's soaked down south too, her wetness making my boxers stick to my flesh.

"I need inside your pussy, doll, or else I'm going to come in my boxers," I manage to rasp before her opposite nipple is thrust into my mouth, effectively shutting me up. I'll happily stop talking if it means I get to play with her gorgeous tits.

Impatient to please her, I immediately begin suckling, using one hand to gently massage her breast at the same time I indulge in her sweetness. Her dainty hand leaves my chin to slide between our bodies. She shoves my underwear down, and in the next beat, she has her panties slid to the side while she glides her cunt over my cock. It feels dirty and naughty and absolutely right. I'm not a small man by any means, which she quickly discovers when she pauses halfway down to draw in a gasp. It's another thing I've always had to worry about, being bigger than average and hurting women. I want to bring pleasure, not pain, and a big cock isn't always as great as it's cracked up to be. I've had issues not being able to fit it into an especially snug cunt before, and I was mortified. Thank fuck I was decent with my tongue.

Swallowing my mouth full of breast milk, I turn away and check in with her. "You okay, Little Momma?"

"Y-you're huge. I'm not trying to build your ego up but you seriously have a big dick."

"I know, beautiful. Take your time. Let yourself adjust to it before you move and hurt your little pussy." One hand moves to her ass, squeezing before my fingers trail under her panties to rub against her ass. My other hand continues to pluck at her nipple, relishing in the milk leaking down her breasts. "You're the sexiest woman I've ever met. I hope you realize that. You're beyond what I was imagining all day today."

"Oh, Spin." She squirms, shifting up, then slamming her hips down. She cries out loudly, making me sit up in a rush to pull her body to my chest and comfort her. I don't want her hurt, by me or anything else.

"Shh, baby. It's okay. I got you." My hand leaves her breast to stroke her hair and back while the other grips her ass cheek tight enough she can't move. "Shh. I got you," I repeat while she draws in a deep soothing breath, then exhales. "We've got forever, Naomi, so take all the time you need. Your pussy feels like straight heaven just resting my cock inside. Makes me think of warm, silky, fluffy clouds."

"A good thing, I take it?" She finally sounds normal, if not a little breathy.

"Hell yeah. The best. I wish I could explain it to you better, but it's the best I've ever felt. Never had pregnant pussy before... unless it's just you. I'm crazy over you."

"Never?"

"Nah, I haven't been with many women," I admit, feeling a bit embarrassed about it for some reason. I've been around men who've basically slept their way through a continent, bragging about it constantly, but that's never been me. Not to mention, my looks have turned women away—I'm assuming so, anyhow. Women don't want an intimidating man that doesn't fit into the basic mold of Joe-Shmoo down the road.

"That only makes me want you even more."

My chest rumbles with satisfaction. She likes the fact I haven't been with many others, and she's riding my cock right now? I must be doing something right. But then again, it is dark and the middle of the night, maybe she kept the lights off on purpose. "Yeah? It doesn't seem odd since I'm closing in on forty?"

She shakes her head, leaning in to press her lips to mine. We slowly rock together, me making her go slow so she doesn't hurt herself again. I swear she did that shit on purpose to test me, to see how I'd react. I'd never rush her or force her to be in any discomfort, though. She holds the reins completely. I don't care what any guy claims—we can always stop and we can always wait, no questions asked. If a man isn't willing to do that, he's the wrong type of man. Women deserve to be respected and coveted, whether it's the first night I'm meeting her or the hundredth.

"I had to feel your cock inside me or else I was going to come from you milking me."

Fuck. My cock pulses at her choice of words. She may be a sweet little thing in the daylight, but she's a freak in the sheets, and I'm loving every minute of it. "You and me both, beautiful. How you feeling? Your pussy hurting too badly?" She's drenched my cock, so she must be feeling better.

"Oh, Spin, it's so good. I want to bounce on your dick. Can I?"

"Of course. You never have to ask. It's all yours, Naomi." And I mean every word. *It's hers—I'm hers.* I'm such a goner and have no idea how it could've ever happened so fast. I still can't believe this is real, that Naomi is this perfect for me.

Lying back again, I grasp her breast in my left hand once more while she begins to move. Naomi rides my length like a damn stripper pole, making me gasp with each tight stroke. There's no way I'll last long like this, so I do the only thing I can think of to even the playing field a bit. My hand slides to her ass crease, finding her back entrance. She draws in a swift breath when the tip of my finger toys with her opening. Moaning loudly, her pussy gushes fresh wetness, strangling my cock, and I know she's about to let go.

On her next downward stroke, my middle finger slides in her backdoor in one long stroke. She screams, "Spin!" long and loud as she comes, the sounds and sensations sending me spiraling into my own orgasm. I roar through my release, filling her with my cum.

It's so intense I know I'm ruined for anyone else.

And damn straight!

I want to impregnate her with my baby next.

***

Sleepily, I peel my lids open, realizing Naomi's on her side, snuggled up to my chest, her baby bump comfortably nestled against my flank, making me feel some type of way first thing in the morning. I want to feel her silkiness on my fingertips, but if I stroke her skin, I may wake her, and the thing she needs the most right now is rest. I still can't get over the fact she traveled this far alone without knowing she had a place to go.

She's brave.

Far braver than what's good for her.

She should've called the cops on her piece of shit ex and his father and had them both arrested, then called Sadie to make sure the club would take her. It's easy to think that way and judge when you're not in the other person's shoes, though. I'm sure if she felt she had another choice, she'd have gone about things differently. To have to leave her home and almost all her belongings behind, it must be taking a toll on her emotionally. She's about to have a baby and literally has nothing for the child or herself. Christmas is coming next week too, and I can only imagine how sad she may feel because of the holiday. I don't want her to worry and be gloomy. I need to figure out a way to make sure she's smiling now and in the future.

The only thing I can think of is I have a small apartment above my tattoo shop. We need to keep her here to make sure she's safe, but maybe in a few months, she'd like to stay there. I could fix it up for her and the baby, and if she's not comfortable with me staying there too, I can sleep downstairs in my shop on the couch. I'm crazy for thinking about this already—I barely know the woman, yet I feel like I've been waiting my entire life for her.

I'll take it one day at a time. First off, today, I'm heading to our H-E-B to pick up the things Cain told me to grab. Thankfully, that store seems to have a bit of everything. If they have any cool baby stuff, I'll grab it too and drop it by my shop to hide until Christmas. There's no way I'm allowing her to spend the holiday here and not have her wake up to a few gifts. We've done similar in the past with the other women who stayed at the club by throwing them baby showers. This is different, though. It's me doing it all because I want to.

Should I climb out of bed and leave her to sleep in? Or wait until she wakes up? She doesn't know anyone, so I don't want her to be uncomfortable or think I bailed after what happened in the middle of the night. It was the last thing I ever expected but I'm not complaining. On the contrary, I was over the moon I got to sink balls deep in her tight cunt. She was heaven and sin all wrapped up in a sexy package, riding my cock like it belonged to her. *Fuckin' a-mazing.*

Having made up my mind, I lightly stroke the pad of my finger along her brow and press a kiss to the top of her head. She smells like me, being all wrapped up in my scent. I've never felt more pride than right now, having this stunning woman in my arms. My touch trails lower, moving over her lips, grinning when they turn up into a sleepy smile. "Good morning, beautiful."

"Mmm… a woman could get used to being woken up like this."

"I hope so," I quietly murmur and kiss her hair again. I hope she's not ashamed of fucking me last night once she gets a good look at me this morning. I don't have my contact in, so my iris will be completely black, and my hair's all jacked from bedhead. *Will she still find me attractive like yesterday? Or was that just a sexual need fueling her touch?*

Her hand tucks around my hip, snuggling into my frame. "You're so warm and comfortable. I usually toss and turn to get comfortable with my belly, but it fits perfectly against you." Her thumb strokes my flesh, giving me goose bumps. Quietly she asks, "Does that weird you out?"

"The opposite. I'm glad you slept good and even more so that it was because you found comfort in me." My voice is deeper than usual, raspy from sleep, and with that toss in some added emotion.

Her belly fits perfectly with me… just like I think she does.

I can't help but imagine how different things would be right now if she were having my baby. *Whoever hurt her makes me want to hurt them.*

Brushing the thoughts away, I continue, "I'm going to get up and run an errand. You're welcome to take a shower, and feel free to borrow whatever you need of mine. If you want to eat, help yourself in the kitchen. Sadie will be around, and she'll need you to use her online accounts to get some pictures of everyone we should be keeping an eye out for. She usually makes multiple prints so we all have a copy in case someone looks out of place. We have a few local businesses who keep an eye out too, so they can give us a heads up."

"I can't believe they're willing to do that," she says, glancing up to meet my stare. She's adorable in her mussed, just-woken-up look.

"Of course they are. We've helped many of them out a time or two."

"You really are the good guys, huh?" Her gaze shines with something I'm not able to read, but I like the look while it's directed my way.

"We're not, doll. We're one percenters, not the fluffy weekender riders you see out and about. This is our way of life. However, we do help our community and women who request it. I'll never stand by idly while a woman is hurt by anyone and asks for help. I don't care if I die trying. She'll have someone on her side."

"You may not be the good guys, Spin, but you're a damn good man. Thank you for coming to my rescue."

"Anytime, baby. You can count on it." I kiss her forehead, and she leans up to press one to my mouth. I wasn't going to go there unless she showed me she was cool with it. With the green light from her, I kiss her twice more, not getting enough. "I gotta get out of here or I'll never leave. Say, do you like chocolate?"

She snorts. "Spin. I'm hella pregnant,'" she quotes my words back to me. "I *love* chocolate. The milkier and smoother, the better."

Christ, the word milk falling from her perfect mouth is going to give me a fucking boner. Jumping out of bed, I flash her a grin and head for the bathroom to take a piss and wash up.

I have to get out of here, or my earlier sentiment will ring true, and we'll never leave this room.

CHAPTER SEVEN

Naomi

"The Christmas trees are magical. The guys don't mind there being so many?"

Sadie chuckles, shaking her head. "They tried to grumble about it, but it didn't last for long. Too many ol' ladies wanting to pitch in their touches around here to bring in some holiday spirit. Don't tell a soul I shared this with you, but pussy runs this house, not dick."

A laugh bubbles up, not expecting her to say that. "Well, that's refreshing. Do the guys know it too or just the women?"

Her smile's wide as she says, "They think they run it, but we know the truth." She winks, making me snicker again. "You'll meet everyone over the next week with it being Christmas. This is the best time to be at the club, in my opinion. Lots of cooking, hanging out, and having fun together. There's always a full house for the holiday. Think of us as one big family you get to be welcomed into."

She's seriously the sweetest person I've met so far, aside from Spin. I had a brief encounter this morning with Avery and Ares. They were in the kitchen when Sadie was giving me the official tour. They were nice but didn't talk much. I'm the new one around here though, so they probably need time to warm up to me. Sadie's ol' man, Twist, is here too, even though I haven't seen him yet. According to her, he spends the majority of his time out in the garage, especially when the weather is cool. She said that he and Spin build bikes together. Well, Twist builds them and Spin custom paints them.

The printer stops, spitting out several of the same copy. Sadie stands from behind the desk and grabs the pictures. "Okay, I think we have what we need. I'm going to pass these around the club and make sure other significant places get them. Have you thought about filing a police report to request a restraining order? Or have you done that already?"

Shaking my head, my hands fist as nervous tremors begin to overtake them. I refuse to be a trembling mess in front of her, and clenching my hands helps make it stop for the time being. Probably not healthy bottling it up, but we'll deal with those issues another day. Right now, I have to fight through the anxiety of the thoughts of potential future abuse give me. "They'll find out my location if I get a restraining order. It's too late for me to file a report. Plus, I don't want anyone to see anything coming from Texas. I want to become a ghost, if possible. Just disappear for them to never find me."

"I understand, but it could help if these guys come looking to hurt you. A paper trail is good when it comes to justice being served."

Shaking my head, I hold back my snort of disbelief where justice comes into play with abusers. I've seen how many women end up hospitalized or dead from filing reports and nothing being done by the police. Trust me, I researched all about it before deciding what the best plan would be for me. "It's not good when my safety is in jeopardy, though."

She nods. "I get it. More so than others. Don't worry. We'll make it through this together, and you'll be able to live a happy life without these bastards ruining it for you. They ever show up here, they're in for one hell of an awakening."

"Thank you. I keep repeating my gratitude to you, but I feel it's never truly enough. Someday, I hope to repay your kindness however I can."

She waves me off. "Nonsense. The fact I can help in any way is payment enough. Helping feeds my soul with light."

Before I give myself the chance to overthink it, I spring forward, wrapping her in a firm hug. My emotions are spiking, my throat feeling tight with the potential onslaught of tears about to burst free. If I'm ever in the position to help another as they're doing for me here, I'll pay it forward. Everyone out there deserves to have this kind of safety and kindness in their lives. "Also, ah… am I allowed to like Spin?"

After she squeezes me back, she steps away, her face screwed up in amusement. "Like Spin? You can like anyone you want. No one will tell you any differently, and if they do, tell them to take a hike." She's so tiny but feisty and I love her energy.

"I mean as in… crushing on him. It seems *so* bad when I think of it. I'm running from a family of jerks, and boom, twitterpated with this sexy biker. I promise I'm not a hoe. I don't make it a habit of wanting someone after only a day or while being pregnant by another baby daddy."

"I'm not judging, promise, and no one here will either. I'm pretty confident you're not the only one with a crush. Spin was flashing you serious puppy-dog eyes yesterday when he introduced us."

My smile's wide enough that it makes my cheeks hurt. "So you're saying Santa may give me a biker for Christmas?"

She nods, giggling. "I already like you, Nay. I seriously hope you stick around after you have the baby and everything has calmed down."

My smile relaxes as I release a heavy breath. "I hope I'm able to. I've met more kind people here since I arrived than I have in the last month where I used to live. I see why so many people love it down here."

"Eh, we'll see if you're still saying that when summer rolls around. On the upside, no snow shoveling."

"See? Sold already." I grin as a good-looking biker interrupts us.

"Sade's, you about done with the printer?"

She nods. "This is Naomi." Then gestures to the man I briefly saw last night when I went to find Spin in the bar. "Nay, this is my brother, 2 Piece."

"Like brother-brother or MC kind?"

He smirks, his bright blue eyes stunning me with their color. "I'm her older brother. By DNA and everything. It's just a bonus for her that she also gets to live by me."

Sadie rolls her eyes and flips him the bird. "Pay no attention to my brother. If his head gets any bigger, he won't be able to fit through the doorway."

She tucks her arm in mine, pulling me with her as I laugh. "Nice meeting you, 2 Piece," I call as we head for the main area and bar. He was cute and seemed friendly. I can get along with easy-going people really well, and he rubbed me as having that type of personality. "He has the most beautiful blue eyes."

"He knows it too. Not only does he have one partner, but two. He's with Ares and Avery."

My mouth pops open, stunned. "Two people?" *The same people I met today?*

"Yep. Been together for years. I wanted to give you a heads-up because you'll see them all together or with one or the other. I didn't want you to get the wrong impression that they're not being faithful or whatever. They are all committed to each other." She watches me a bit, and I get the feeling it's some sort of test. I'm open-minded, though, so it's no big deal to me whatever others choose to do.

Not knowing what the right response is, I go with what comes naturally to me. "Good for them. Some people can't find one person to love, but they've all managed to find two. Pretty cool."

"It is cool." She nods, pride shining brightly for her brother and his mates. "You'll find that around here, folks are a lot more accepting toward everyone. We may give each other a hard time and tease each other, but we never outright judge anyone. Everyone has a background and some sort of story we may not know about, so we approach it with open hearts. If you can do as much, you'll fit in just fine around here."

"Well, hearing you say that definitely puts my mind more at ease on the Spin matter, as well as me showing up and not knowing anyone. I'm not the type to go off and randomly judge people, ever. I don't do that unless someone is ugly to me right off the bat. Then it's hard for me not to think they have a poor attitude on life and in general."

"Good. Like I said... I already like you." She flashes me a wink, and I grin. I have a feeling we're going to be good friends, and I sure hope my intuition is right because I like her too. "Now I need to talk to Spin about getting a tree for his room. You need one of your own to decorate and make his room feel a bit more festive and welcoming."

"Oh no, nothing extra. Food and shelter are more than I could ever imagine. Then throwing in safety... what you've offered is already priceless, in my opinion." A deep pain hits me as I finish, and my hand shoots to my stomach. Cradling the large ball making up my belly, I exhale and breathe through the lingering pains. "Ouch."

"Are you okay? What hurts?"

"I got a sharp pain."

"Did the baby kick hard or shift?"

Shaking my head, I inhale and exhale again, collecting myself. "No, it just hurt suddenly."

"I don't like it. Let's get you in bed and prop your feet up. You're supposed to be resting this week, and I'm towing you all around the clubhouse, stressing you out."

"I've been enjoying myself, though. I appreciate you taking the time. I'm sure you have plenty of other things you could be doing."

She waves me off, taking my elbow to direct me toward the hall with Spin's room. "My kids are in school right now, so it's no problem at all. Besides, my ol' man always drops them off and picks them up."

"You haven't mentioned anything about them. How old are they? Is Twist involved a lot... if you don't mind me asking, that is?"

Her irises light up as she says, "My oldest is in sixth grade, and the youngest is in kindergarten. Twist is an amazing father. I couldn't ask for more. He's extremely protective of our children and involved with everything."

"You're lucky. I worry about mine growing up with no father and no strong male figure to lead them down the right path. It's also scary to not have anyone I can turn to for help I may eventually need."

"You don't know if your baby won't have a father, so stay optimistic. Who knows, you could fall head over heels for someone out of the blue. As for not having anyone, you have an entire club of people willing to be here for you. Let us help."

Nodding, I chew on the inside of my cheek. The fact that she wants to help and seems so genuine about it throws me for a loop. These seem to be the people I've needed to be around for my entire life. I'm so grateful to have found them, not only for myself but for my child and our future as well.

"Come on, lady. Let's get you back in bed." She opens Spin's door for me, and I step inside. It's the same as I left it, the air still smelling like Spin. I used his body wash and his spray deodorant, and I can't seem to escape from his scent now. It's stronger in here and has me wanting to breathe deeply to get my fix of him.

Climbing onto the bed, I watch as she grabs the blanket from the chair and rolls it up, stuffing it under my ankles. I would never have thought to use the blanket like this. It's a good thing I'm around someone who has been through what I'm experiencing. Pregnancy is a learning process, and no two days in a row are the same, it seems. "Thank you."

"No problem. Keep your feet up for a while so they don't swell too bad and drink some water. Try to take a nap, and no stressing allowed."

Chuckling, I nod. "You have my word."

"Good. I'll hold you to it. See you later, and let us know if you need anything." She does a finger wave as she closes the door behind her, leaving me in silence.

Coming here seems too good to be true. *Should I doubt it or count my blessings?* And Spin—Jesus did I hit the jackpot with that guy. I don't mean monetary wise, but by care and compassion. I thought I'd met every type of person out there in the world by now, but he took me by complete surprise. Now the hard part—not falling for him and getting a different body part hurt, my heart. I can already tell he can easily steal it in a flash, should he wish to.

A man who is kind, caring, respectful, gorgeous, protective, and happens to have a huge dick?

Unicorn.

I'd believed up until now those types of men didn't exist, but Spin clearly proves my theory all wrong. And I want him for all of it.

I could take off this very moment and do my own thing out in the world, but not only does the safety of my unborn child worry me, but now I'm sensing some sort of anchor cementing me to Spin. I don't want to run further away from my problems and leave him behind. I need to see where things can go with the sexy biker.

Crazy, right? Meeting someone and falling face first into lust and possibly love with them all in a day? It seems absolutely impossible, and it should be, but then, you've never met this guy before. He's the ultimate game-changer, the guy who makes you want to be a better woman for. You always hear of men saying they meet a woman who makes them want to be better—well, he has that same effect. On me.

Eventually, I doze off for a bit, and when I wake again, he's back. Not only is he looking every bit of the gorgeous outlaw with his tall, dark mohawk and different-colored eyes, but he's come bearing gifts. He proudly shows me the flannel-covered body pillow, fluffy sherpa robe, fuzzy slippers a size too big, mini massager, gel eye compress, shea tummy butter, pregnancy magazine, a bag full of snacks, and a bottle of chocolate milk.

"You bought all this…" I pause, swallowing as tears crest, "… for me? Why?"

"Because I want you to be comfortable. Happy."

A tear trickles over my cheek while I fight to hold my sob in. I will not lose control of my emotions and break down crying like a crazy person in front of this wonderfully sweet man. I refuse to lose it when he wants me happy. But I am. I may have a tear falling from my jaw right now, but it's from my happiness. The feeling that Spin has given me and no other. Not to this degree. Him and I, we must be meant for something more together for me to feel this type of way for him.

Everything that's happened, I have to believe it was all leading me to this moment.

To him.

Hopping out of bed, I throw myself at Spin, leaping as high as I can to toss my arms around him in the biggest hug I can manage. I'm on the cusp of losing my shit. I need this hug just as much as I want him to feel my gratitude. The fact he went out of his way for me two days in a row, and not only by little bits either. He's shown me the type of person he is. The sort of man he'd help me raise my son to be. I've never trusted my gut more than I do in this moment—my intuition is screaming that he's *the one*.

Who am I to fight fate? I asked the world for help, for a sign, and it's given me one in the last place I ever expected to find it.

"Thank you. You have made me a very happy woman. Let me show you how much." I tug his neck down as I pop up on my tiptoes. My lips meet his, and the room begins to twist around us. There's nothing but him and me, and the rest is whatever we allow it to be. In here, it's our electric lust mixed with feelings far too strong to ignore. I don't have to hide from him, and he doesn't have to hold back from me. It's our special nest. Our home together. At least I hope it will be.

"I need you in me," I whisper against his mouth in between kisses, impatient to feel him over me and inside, warming me everywhere. My body's practically vibrating with desire for him. Surely he can feel it too. "Please make me yours, Spin?"

"You were mine the moment I found you." He quietly admits, walking me backward to his bed. My shirt goes first, and he tosses it onto the comforter. Next is his, as he reaches behind his neck and tugs it over his head in that sexy weird way men always do. He's not overly muscular, more like defined. His wingspan is long, arms are nicely sculpted with muscles and thick veins. Probably from all the riding and tattooing he's done for most of his life. His stomach doesn't have a six-pack or anything, but it doesn't stick out either. It's the type of tummy I could lay my head on and be comfortable enough to fall asleep, yet tug his jeans down a touch and see the sexy V leading me to what I want to taste next.

CHAPTER EIGHT

Spin

Popping the button on my jeans free, my lips tip into a sinful smirk as I push her pants down. Without any hesitation, mine are shoved off next. I'm so fucking eager, ready to feel skin-on-skin contact and explore. I hope Naomi's as impatient as I am—so far, she seems to be. We were together in the dark last night, but now I finally get to see all of her voluptuous perfection in the light, and it has my mouth watering with anticipation.

My plan to grab her a few things went a bit overboard because I got excited. In no way was I expecting her to jump my bones the moment she saw it all. I won't be turning her away, though. This is one hell of a treat I'll gladly take, so long as she offers. Glancing over her body, a low whistle escapes me. "So fine, doll. I could stare all day." And that cute little belly of hers only makes me more turned on than ever. I want to fuck her, then fuck her again, and fill her with my cum.

Being the respectful individual I am, I ask, "Can I come inside you, Little Momma? I promise I'm clean." We didn't exactly work this shit out in the middle of the night, so I want her to know upfront. She never has to worry about me harming her in any way.

"Yes, I want you to fill me up."

My eyes about bug out at her words—a man's dream come true. "Christmas came early for me," I mumble, my knees hitting the end of the bed. I have all kinds of crazy positions I want to stick her in, but I'm trying to take it easy on her body right now.

"Because you get warm, wet, and willing pussy?"

Ten Minutes

"Fuckin' shit," I curse, sweat dotting my brow. She has a way with words, that much is certain. "I meant in the form of you, but your pussy is a damn fine present as well."

"Aww, you seriously say some of the sweetest things at random times."

Shrugging, I offer her a grin and trail kisses up the inside of her leg. Pause to bite the flesh beside her knee and make her giggle, then continue my exploration. She has the type of body I could worship for hours. All curves and softness. I'm practically foaming at the mouth to see her titties bounce while I'm driving deep. My tongue finds her clit, making her moan loudly. My nuts tighten at the sinful sound, my cock throbbing. I could drive deep in one thrust, her cunt's so wet. I don't want to hurt her, but someday I'll have her stretched out enough she will beg for me to slam home.

Her thighs begin to shake as I slide two of my fingers in and out of her entrance, spreading her wetness around so she's ready for my cock. My tongue fondles her precious bundle of sensitive nerves, sucking and slurping until she's yanking my hair and screaming my name. Her taste floods my mouth as I eagerly lick her juices, her flavor setting me into a deeper lustful frenzy for her.

Licking my lips, I wipe her wetness from my jaw as I scoot up until my thighs kiss the backs of her legs. Grabbing my length, I run it up and down her slit, loving how she thrashes, begging me to put it in. "Soon, sexy momma, soon." Continuing to play, I roll my hips a bit until my tip barely presses to her hole, then out again. I repeat the move over and over until Naomi's begging me to make her come again.

"Spin, put it inside. I want to feel you in me. Fill me up," she demands, and I do as I'm told. With slow, careful strokes, I shove in to the hilt, careful to brace my weight off of her frame. She needs to lie back and enjoy herself while I make sure she has another orgasm. I want to be her man, and as her man, it's my job to satisfy her always.

Reaching forward, I cup her jaw and ask, "Can I be your man, baby?" She's so gorgeous like this, vulnerable and open for the taking.

"You want to be mine?"

Nodding, I push forward, then back. "More than anything. I want to be yours, and I want you to be mine. I won't pressure you, and I promise to be good to you," I whisper, leaning in to kiss her tenderly.

"Please don't hurt me, Spin," she says with a heavy breath.

"Never. You have my word. I'll care for you and the baby. You don't ever have to worry again," I promise, making my way down her jaw to kiss her neck. "I'll keep you safe." I begin to suck, listening to her speak.

"You don't think it's too soon? It's all happening so fast."

"I know. It is for me too. That's why we're going to take it one day at a time. You good with being together but taking it slow between us? No expectations involved, just two people who enjoy each other's company and want to be together." I can't believe I'm the one asking this and bombarding her with it all while we're in the middle of having sex. I can't hold back anymore, though. I need to know she wants the same thing I do before I get sucked in too deep. I'm already so far gone that she has me wanting to claim her on her second day here. I can only imagine how much more invested I'll get if she doesn't pump the brakes on me right now and tell me to back off. I don't think I can be just fuck buddies with her. I'm invested and want her too badly—it'd crush me, attempting to shut my emotional side down. Or God forbid I wait it out, hoping she changes her mind, and end up strung along with a wrecked heart at the end of it all.

Her hands move to hold my cheeks, making me meet her intense stare. She leans up, pressing her mouth to mine, kissing me, and then muttering the sweet sound I want to hear, "I'm good with taking it slow between us, with being together. I feel lucky to have met you. Thank you for coming into my life, Spin."

"I'm the lucky one."

***

"What's wrong?" I ask, taking in her pained expression the following day. It instantly has me on edge and ready to do whatever I can to take it away.

"It hurts."

"What does, doll? Tell me whatever you can so I can try to help."

"My stomach, the baby. Something's wrong." Tears cloud her gaze as I grab her jacket, stuffing her into it. She doesn't strike me as the type to complain unless it's truly serious. She's been so strong and hardheaded thus far that witnessing the fear in her expression has my breath stuttering.

"Everything will be okay, Naomi. Don't worry. We'll go to the doctor, and they'll fix whatever is going on."

She catches my hands, making me pause. "W-what if they can't?"

"I don't accept that possibility, and neither should you. The kid is causing a bit of mischief, is all. We'll get it sorted. Grab on to my neck."

"Spin, I can walk!"

"Nope. Grab on," I argue stubbornly, leaving no room for disagreement.

Her arms loop around my neck, tightening to hold on as I lift her and powerwalk through the club. "I need keys!" I shout as soon as I hit the doorway to the bar.

Twist and Sadie both leap from the table they are sitting at.

"Oh shit," Twist mumbles, tossing a set of keys my way. I barely manage to catch them one-handed, not willing to release my hold on Naomi. "Take 2 Piece's truck. He won't mind. Let us know what's up."

I nod, and Sadie yells as we're leaving through the main door, "Text if you need anything at all. I mean it!"

The door slams behind us as I hurriedly trek to the truck, attempting not to jostle Naomi too much, but also scared for her and wanting to haul ass at the same time. "You hanging in there? You haven't made a peep since I picked you up."

"Just concentrating on breathing and feeling the baby move. As long as there's movement, there is hope."

"Chin up, babe. There's always hope. You just stay calm, and we'll see the doc soon."

She doesn't respond, her mouth tipped down as she watches our path. Opening the passenger side truck door, I carefully set her inside, pausing long enough to buckle the belt. I know she's more than capable of doing it herself, but she's frightened, and I want to take care of her as long as she'll allow me to. Jogging around the front of the truck, I hop in the driver's side and crank the engine, forgoing my own belt. Once we get out the gate, with a quick honk at the prospect, I wrap the belt over my torso and buckle it, stepping on the gas.

Hauling ass, I ignore the speed limits, only concerned about getting to the hospital before it's too late for whatever is going on in Naomi's belly. The cops around here tend to leave this vehicle, as well as our others, alone. We do a lot to help them out on the down-low anytime they need it, and in return, they usually leave us in peace for the most part.

We make it to the hospital much quicker than the ambulance had on the last trip, and I'm silently thanking our lucky stars for time being on our side today. "I got you, Little Momma," I grumble, hopping back out of the truck as soon as I pull it in a spot and slam the gear shift in park, barely remembering to turn the damn thing off before I bail.

Opening her door, she instantly snuggles into my arms, allowing me to carry her inside. I think she realizes I'm not having it any other way right now. The last thing she needs is any stress on this body at all.

"My woman's in pain. She's pregnant, and we need help right away," I call as soon as we're through the automatic doors.

"Please," Naomi tacks on to the end for good measure.

The desk lady rushes behind a wall, and in a flash, two nurses quickly stride our way. One grabs a wheelchair, and the other stops beside us to ask basic questions. She peppers my woman with them, and Naomi answers each one, all the while I stand here looking like a fish out of water.

"Sir." The other nurse interrupts my blank stare, calling my attention. "Sir," she repeats. "Momma and baby are going to be fine. We'll take care of her. Follow us back and we'll put her in a room. Just stay with us, Dad."

She thinks I'm the father? I bounce a swift glance in Naomi's direction as the nurse wheels her down the hallway. She holds her hand out to me, and I grab it, wanting to comfort her. She doesn't correct the nurse's assumption, so I don't either. Let them believe I'm the father. Whatever will ensure me access to my woman and finding out what's going on. I just found her, and I'm damn sure not letting her go.

She's helped onto the hospital bed, and not by me, much to my chagrin. They wrap a stretchy pink belt around her belly, which they promise me won't hurt either of them, and in a flash, beeps and lines start up from a monitor next to the bed.

"See this?" One of them points. "Baby has a strong heartbeat."

75

"So does Momma." The other reassures, meeting my concerned stare for a beat. She moves to set up an IV in Naomi's hand while continuing to ask her questions. I don't know what any of them mean, talking about timing between pain, fluid leaking, and other stuff that only serves to freak me the fuck out. If only I'd known sooner I'd be helping have a baby, I'd have researched it online or something.

"The baby is coming?" I murmur, my thoughts going haywire. I need them to give me an hour to find some videos on what to expect.

The nurse who reassured me before—her name tag says Sarah—offers a soft expression. She knows it's too early and this is bad news.

I'm freaking the fuck out.

"We're going to check her further, as will the doctor. To be frank, I think she's in premature labor. It's okay, though. The doctor will make sure Naomi and the baby get some meds to slow things down. We want the baby to stay in her belly for as long as possible." I feel like she's having to dumb it down a bunch for me to understand what exactly is going on, but I appreciate it. I'd be lost if she talked to me in the same terms the other lady has been using with Naomi.

The only thing that matters to me right here, right now… is that Naomi and the baby make it through this just fine, and I can take my new family back home. I have so much more time I need to spend with them both. Panic builds in my chest at the thought of something harming either of them, and my vision grows spotty.

"Sir?" is shouted, but it sounds like I'm underwater. "Oh shit, grab him before he falls. He needs to lie down. The dads always pass out."

76

EPILOGUE

Naomi
One Year Later...

The smile on my face is wider than usual because I have a surprise for Spin. A Christmas gift he won't be expecting. Sadie knows, but of course, she does. She's quickly become my closest friend over the last year. I love the other ol' ladies around here too, but Sadie will always hold a special place in my heart for what she's done to help women in the world who are scared and struggling. She gave me hope in a time I was too frightened to have any.

And then there's Spin.

The man is my entire world, aside from our daredevil almost-one-year-old.

I learned a lot about him over the past year. For example, my big guy has some serious confidence issues. Had we not been thrust into living together right off the bat, I don't know if I'd have ever discovered as much. He's never allowed anyone in the past to get close enough to see his vulnerabilities, but he had no choice with me, aside from basically kicking me out. Thank God he wasn't going to let that happen under any circumstance. Once I figured out what he was dealing with internally, I was able to reinforce his confidence, and we were able to heal together. I thought he was beautiful from the moment he walked into my hospital room, but to see him grow over the past year alongside me has been amazing, and I'm so happy I could do something in return for all the things he's done for us as well. I've become completely smitten with him, and so has my baby.

Christmas music blares throughout the room as London and several of the club kids dance around, smiling and giggling, having a great time together. Watching them and experiencing the sense of belonging I have here is an unexplainable feeling. These people have become my family—the ones I can rely on and enjoy being around. I never imagined a biker club full of everything I needed would be at the end of my road, but here it is, and I couldn't be happier. If it weren't for Spin taking me in, for wanting to help me, I'd have none of this now. Every time I attempt to remind him and thank him, he shuts me down, claiming I belong here as much as anybody else.

However, if Spin hadn't found me on the road over a year ago and essentially saved me, there's no telling what could've happened to me. A dark place inside believes I'd be dead, but I try not to go there often as it brings my mood down. I've learned to be thankful for everything I've been offered and to embrace the here and now, not dwell in the past. It's one thing I had to get used to with the Oath Keepers—they live in the present as they claim every day is a gift not meant to waste. It's freeing in a sense, not worrying about the future but taking it day by day.

Spin had promised me when he asked me to be his that we'd take it slow, and he's held true to his word. I've never felt pressured or like I'm a burden to him in any way. Did you know there are men out there who are truly patient, kind, and understanding? Threw me for a loop too, but they do exist, and they're positively glorious to spend your life with.

"Mama mama," my kiddo babbles, grabbing onto my leg. My heart has never felt fuller than it does now. Being a mother is the best thing in the entire world. Having Spin by my side is the second.

When I went into labor early last Christmas, I was positively terrified. Spin was too. I'll never forget the moment he squeezed my hand and bowed his head. He'd said, "I'm not the prayin' type, doll, but I need whatever help I can get to make sure you and that kid are all right." I'd gained a newfound respect for him. The fact he'd cared so much about us so quickly, well, it said all I needed to know about him as a man. I was already crazy for him, but in that very moment, I knew I was going to love him for the rest of my life.

We'd prayed together, asking for help from anyone out there willing to listen and lend a hand. I've never been the type of woman needing to be saved before last year, and thankfully, Spin has this habit of being around right when I need him to be. So when he prayed, I thanked the universe for sending him to me because without him, I'm not so sure I would make it.

I'd gotten an IV with some medicine to help slow the labor down and also some steroid shots to give the baby a boost in case I went into labor again. Eventually, the contractions stopped. I wasn't in pain anymore, and we were both okay.

Since then, Spin has become the "praying type." Even if it's simply to say thank you each morning for allowing him to wake up to us for one more day, he's murmuring a little prayer. I can't imagine a better role model for my little mini than Spin.

I know now he was the one who found me for a reason.

My soul called to his, and he answered.

Once things were back to being okay after the almost-early labor, and I was feeling better, he still wouldn't let me walk. He was ridiculously stubborn, and I may have called him a caveman several times, but he was determined I had the healthiest pregnancy possible. When he had to go on runs for the club, he always had Sadie stay with me, and he'd call home several times a day to check on me. I still had my son early, but thankfully, he got to spend a little more time in my tummy to grow. At that point, every day counted, and we were grateful for each one we got.

It's a different world entirely when a man loves you with every breath he takes. I didn't know what to do with that kind of strong love at first, but now I never want to live my days without it.

"Drink your juice." I hold the sippy cup of half water and half apple juice to him. We're transitioning to sippy cup full time, and my little one isn't sure how to feel about it. However, I can't imagine having multiples drinking out of bottles and in diapers, so we're full-fledged into sippy cups and potty training. From what I've read, we're a little early, but my guy started walking two months ago, so I figure he's already further ahead than the average baby for his age.

It's been fairly easy going so far, as having a boy, they can run around and pee on any tree they see to get started. Luckily, being at the club, no one bats an eye, and London swears it's how Jameson was potty trained. Sadie too with Cyle.

What am I going to do if this next baby is a girl, though? Spin will probably follow her around and mean mug anyone who looks her way, yet be a giant lush when it comes to her. It's going to be amazing. He's turned out to be such a wonderful father already.

"Aunty wants to dance!" Sadie chimes, picking my son up and swinging him around until he squeals and giggles. I grin, watching them until Sadie nods, gesturing behind me.

Drawing in a swift breath, I turn to find Spin quickly approaching. His gaze sparkles at the scene before him, and I have no doubt he'll be reporting back to the guys we're having a dance party out here without them. They've been in church, and we've been taking full advantage, setting everything up for the Christmas party.

"Hi, my love," I greet Spin, making him smirk.

"Doll. You're looking mighty fine over here. Sadie's got little man, so I may have to steal you for a beat."

"Hmm... just a beat? Not high hopes today, eh?" I tease, making him roll his eyes.

"Shush, you," he murmurs, pressing a tender kiss to my lips. "I apologize about church on Christmas. It's normally not like this."

"No, don't worry about it. We've been busy out here. Besides, you guys can't help it when stuff randomly pops up."

He nods. "You're good to me, Little Momma. Look, I know the kids already tore through their gifts and we were waiting to open ours until later, but I don't want to put mine off any longer."

A grin breaks free and I nod. I've been vibrating with excitement over exchanging gifts with him. His hold drops from around me to grab my hand and tug me toward the big tree off in the corner. This morning, it was full of gifts for all the club brats. They were so excited. It was adorable. We made pancakes and hung out, and it was probably one of the best Christmas mornings I've ever experienced.

He pulls a large craft garment box out that'd been tucked toward the back. It has a bright green bow and a tag with my name on it. He proudly holds it out to me, and I eagerly take it, flashing him an excited grin. "I wasn't sure if we were going to open ours alone or out here."

"Everyone can see this." He notes, gesturing to the box. "Open it!"

"Okay," I respond with a laugh. I yank the top off, my mouth dropping open in a gasp when my eyes land on what's inside. "Is this what I think it is?" I whisper.

His nod is small, his gaze tender. "It is. You know I love you, that you guys are my world. The club is a big part of my life, and I'd like it if we made it a permanent part of yours too. If you'll be mine, forever."

Sniffling, I set the box on the table nearby and pull the leather jacket free. Turning it around, I take in the patches, tears springing to my eyes.

The ol' lady patch.

The jacket.

Only the lifers have one of these.

The importance isn't lost on me, nor is the significance and devotion Spin is offering by giving me this gift. He's pledging his life to mine, not only before me, but in the eyes of his club. I put this on, and I'm his, and he's mine. Yet, deep in my heart, I already know. I never needed the patch to solidify my commitment to him. I knew from the moment he treated me like he loved me with his whole heart that I'd be his forever. I love this man with every breath I take. That will never change, no matter if I have his jacket on my back, his ring on my finger, and his child in my belly. I'm his.

"I would be honored to wear your patch. I love you." He takes the jacket from me, holding it up so I can see the property patch that screams, "Spin's ol' lady." "It's perfect." I stick my arm out, leaning in so he can help me put it on. Once I'm wrapped in the new leather, he tugs it closed, wearing a wide smile. Leaning in, his mouth takes mine in another toe-curling kiss that I swear has me seeing stars behind my eyelids.

I'm breathless when we finally break free to the sounds of cheers. Everyone hoots and hollers at my jacket, shouting their support of me joining the Oath Keeper family. I have sisters, brothers, nieces, and nephews I never knew I wanted but ended up needing in my life. Spin hasn't only given me love, safety, and shelter, he's offered me hope, happiness, and an entire family.

I'm a rich woman.

Lucky in love.

Thankful and never taking anything for granted.

"My turn now." I practically leap for the tiny gift bag. It's small but stuffed with tissue paper to give the illusion of a full bag. Handing it over, I clench my fists in anticipation. The last month has driven me insane, not being able to mention anything. With Christmas being an important time to us since it's right when we met and got together, I knew I had to wait.

"What could you have gotten me?" He takes one piece of tissue paper out and tosses it over his shoulder, making a few people chuckle in the background. "Tattoo ink? New pens?"

Like I'd buy him those. The man is far too picky about his art supplies for me to even attempt to get what he wants.

He tosses another piece of tissue paper behind him, taking his time, all the while my heart feels like it may pound right out of my chest. "Too light. I'm thinking a gift card. Oh, could it be a coupon book for my favorite things?" He pauses to wink, and I huff.

"Stop stalling, biker, and dig in."

"Hey, can't blame a man for enjoying his gift." He smiles cheekily. If I knew he was such a sucker for a present, I'd have gotten him something small sooner. Now I know for next year, though. Finally, he digs into the bottom. He meets my stare, and his smile drops as his face grows serious. Slowly, he pulls his hand out, fist wrapped around the small white stick. "No way. I want to look, but I'm scared," he admits quietly.

"Aw." My mouth twists into a frown as I step to his body, pressing mine against his. Wrapping my hand around his holding the test, I suggest, "How about we look together? I'm right here, okay?"

He nods and clenches his eyes closed for a second before opening his fist, resting in my much smaller hand. It offers him strength right now, and he needs to know he'll always have me to lean on when he needs it.

"Look, my love," I whisper and watch as his eyes flick down.

They fill with tears as he draws in a breath. He exhales, saying, "Really? I'm not imagining this, right? This is truly happening?" His multi-colored irises find mine, his full of unshed tears while mine escape, rolling down my cheeks.

"It's happening. I'm pregnant with your baby, Spin, and I'm so completely in love with you."

"Fuck, Naomi. You've stolen my soul." His big arms surround me, tucking tightly around my waist as he lifts me to him, embracing me in his love as he plants a blistering kiss on me.

Soulmates.

Forever.

The End

Please leave a review or tell a friend to check out *Ten Minutes* if you enjoyed it. Your referral and kind words are the best motivation out there to keep me writing.

XO - Sapphire

Oath Keepers MC:

If you'd like to learn about all the Oath Keepers MC hybrid chapter you can start here:

Princess (Viking)

Daydream (Nightmare)

Baby (Saint and Sinner)

Chevelle (Mercenary)

Cherry (Odin)

Heathen (Blaze)

Hollywood (Chaos)

Flame (aka Death Dealer - Torch)

Read them for free in Kindle Unlimited - Oath Keepers MC Hybrid Collection Book.

To learn about the Oath Keepers MC original chapter you can start here:

Exposed (Cain)

Relinquish (2 Piece)

Forsaken Control (Ares)

Friction (Twist)

Tease (Snake novella)

Ten Minutes (Spin novella)

Read them for free in Kindle Unlimited - Oath Keepers MC Collection Book.

Books By Sapphire Knight

Oath Keepers MC Series
Exposed
Relinquish
Forsaken Control
Friction
Sweet Surrender – short story in Tease
Ten Minutes – novella

Oath Keepers MC Hybrid Series
Princess
Love and Obey – short story in Tease
Daydream
Baby
Chevelle
Cherry
Heathen
Hollywood
Death Dealer (aka FLAME)

Russkaya Mafiya Series
Secrets
Corrupted
Corrupted Counterparts – short story in Tease
Unwanted Sacri!ces
Undercover Intentions

Dirty Down South Series
Freight Train
3 Times the Heat
Bliss

The Vendetti Famiglia
The Vendetti Empire - Part 1
The Vendetti Queen - Part 2
The Vendetti Seven – Part 3
The Vendetti Coward – Part 4

Ten Minutes
The Vendetti Daddy – Part 5
The Vendetti Devil – Part 6

Harvard Academy Elite
Little White Lies
Ugly Dark Truth

Royal Bastards MC Texas
Opposites Attract/B*stard

Kings of Carnage MC Series
Bash – Vice President
Sterling - Prospect
3rd KOC coming soon!

The Chicago Crew
Gangster
Mad Max

VII Knights MC
Hunter – Nomad

Brotherhood of Darkness
(co-Author with Hilary Storm)
The Order of Obsession
Vow of Vengeance

Complete Standalones
Gangster
Unexpected Forfeit
The Main Event – short story in Tease
Oath Keepers MC Collection
Russian Roulette
Tease – Short Story Collection
Oath Keepers MC Hybrid Collection
Vendetti Duet
Harvard Academy Elite
Viking – free newsletter short story in Newsletter
Dirty Down South Collection

Sapphire Knight
Hunter
Naughty Good Girl
Carnal Addiction

Acknowledgments

My boys—You're my whole world. I love you both, this never changes. I can't express how grateful I am for your support and belief in me. You're quick to tell me that my career makes you proud and that I make you proud. As far as Mom wins go, that one takes the cake, even if I do send 'mom memes.' I love you with every beat of my heart, and I will forever.

My Dogs—You guys are assholes, but I love you so much it makes my heart ache. Please stop barking and chugging water when I'm trying to write.

Editor—Swish Editing & Design. Your hard work makes mine stand out, and I'm so grateful!

My Blogger, Bookstagrammer, and TikTok Friends—YOU ARE AMAZING! You take a new chance on me with each book and, in return, share my passion with the world. You never truly get enough credit, and I'm forever grateful for every share and shout-out.

My Readers—I love you. You make my life possible, so thank you. I can't wait to meet many of you this year and in the future. To those of you leaving me the awesome spoiler-free reviews, you motivate me to keep writing. For that, I'll forever be grateful as this is my passion in life.

And as always, ADOPT DON'T SHOP! Save a life today and adopt from a rescue or your local animal shelter. #ProudDobermanMom #LastHopeDobermanRescue

About the Author:

Sapphire Knight is a Wall Street Journal and *USA Today* Bestselling Author. Her books all reflect what she loves to read herself. She's a Texas girl at heart who's crazy about football and has always possessed a passion for writing. She originally studied psychology and feels that it's added to her drive for writing diverse characters.

Sapphire is the proud mom of two handsome boys and loves to donate to help animals. When she's not busy in her writing cave, she's playing with her three Doberman Pinschers.

www.authorsapphireknight.com

BookBub:
bit.ly/bookbubSK

Newsletter:
https://bit.ly/SapphireNewsletter

Thank you for reading!

Made in the USA
Columbia, SC
18 February 2025

54029254R00050